Handsome *Enough*

A Pride and Prejudice Adaptation

Jen Geigle Johnson

Follow Jen

Some of Jen's other published books

The Duke's Second Chance
The Earl's Winning Wager
Her Lady's Whims and Whimsies
Suitors for the Proper Miss
Pining for Lord Lockhart
The Foibles and Follies of Miss Grace

The Nobleman's Daughter
Two lovers in disguise

Scarlet
The Pimpernel retold

A Lady's Maid

Can she love again?

His Lady in Hiding
Hiding out as his maid.

Spun of Gold
Rumpelstilskin Retold

Dating the Duke
Time Travel: Regency man in NYC

Charmed by His Lordship
The antics of a fake friendship

Tabitha's Folly
Four over-protective brothers

To read Damen's Secret
The Villain's Romance

Follow her Newsletter

Chapter One

Elizabeth and Jane Bennet walked arm in arm from Meryton back to their home at Longbourn, deeply engrossed in their opinions of the local militia who had just come to stay.

Jane dipped her head to allow her bonnet to shield her from the harshest rays of the sun. "I cannot see how Officers Barnes or Cadwell would be anything more than a flirtation for any of us. They have nothing with which to recommend them. And we have no fortunes to recommend *us*. Any ties there will only lead to ruin." Jane's typically positive and sunny personality had taken a strangely dark and pragmatic turn.

"I cannot account for your sudden cynicism, Jane." Lizzy shook her head, but smiled away the pretend censure. "I do have to agree with you. There is no sense in flirting with the officers, but since there is nothing else to do here in our small part of the world, I do see a bit of diversion in it, do you not?"

"Naturally I do, except . . ." She sighed. "It only makes me wish for the same in a true relationship with a true sincerity. I long for a good man who can take me away and save us all from the poorhouse." She spun, clutching her skirts to her.

"What has come over you, dear sister?"

"I think it's those novels you have me reading. You'd think that every woman in the world deserves a dashing fellow who can save her from herself."

"Or lets her be herself." Lizzy pulled her bonnet tighter about her face as the wind picked up. "But back to the officers. I think there is a line of decorum we mustn't cross, lest we make ourselves ridiculous."

Jane nodded. "Certainly we cannot be openly attached to any of them either."

Lizzy felt a ping of personal acknowledgement at that comment, but she brushed her and Wickham's flirtation aside. "Just ask Lydia, who continues to call them only by their first names. Will Father never curb her impropriety?"

"I doubt he will, Lizzy, if he hasn't already."

Elizabeth knew her sister was correct. And she also secretly understood a small part of their younger sister's impropriety. But she would never ever admit just how much she related to her restlessness. “Lydia is bored. We all are. Do *you* not ever simply wish for a meaningless flirtation?” Her gaze flashed to see Jane’s reaction before returning to the path up ahead.

“Lizzy!” Her sister blushed furiously. “How can you think such a thing?”

“I don’t know. It seems easy enough. Take Wickham. Do you not wish to see his eyes loving you as he does the other girls?” She laughed, a warm shiver rushing up her spine before she could stop it. “He will toy with their hair, holds their hands longer than necessary. He speaks so closely to their faces at times.” She fanned herself. “Even if I never hear the man speak, I notice these things. There’s a reason the girls blush.”

“Eyes loving me. Lizzy, I might need to plug my ears. Stop.”

“I will not. I’m just having a bit of fun. He would never be a sincere consideration, would he? He doesn’t look at life seriously. He has no money, which doesn’t matter too much, but it should. What would we eat, for goodness sakes?” But even as she said the words, his laughing eyes mocked her rebellious heart. Because she’d flirted, and a bit more, with the handsome Wickham. She’d felt that lingering touch on her fingers, at her wrist. But no one could know. For they both knew it could go no further. She sighed.

"What is this?" Jane eyed her. "Are you pining away for Mr. Wickham? My glorious Elizabeth, caught in the snares of such a man?"

"No snares." She smiled. "But perhaps a bit caught." She giggled. "Oh, but it's all nonsense. And it will come to nothing." She shrugged. "I find it tiresome that we cannot enjoy a man, have a friend, even—spend time with a person without it having to mean something all the time."

"I know we wish to marry for love and perhaps some form of living, but to marry for a flirtation?" Jane frowned.

"I'm not talking of *marrying* the man." She looked away. This conversation had suddenly become everything she did not wish to think about. It was much more delicious to fall for a bit of abandon now and again, consequences aside. "And there isn't anyone else, is there?"

"Not at the moment, no." Then Jane, usually the most optimistic of people, joined Elizabeth in her sighing.

Before Elizabeth could attempt to cheer her, the sounds of horses coming at fast speeds approached.

"Goodness, that doesn't sound good, does it?" Jane clutched Elizabeth's arm as they hurried off to the side of the road.

The horses rounded a bend, magnificent animals. Men in top hats and breeches sat astride, laughing, one dark, the other light, their shoulders broad, their jaws sharp. They were gentlemen indeed, and quite handsome. She lifted a hand to alert them of their presence, but neither seemed to notice. Their horses galloped forward as though no one else were there. Jane and Elizabeth inched back as far as they could for the trees. Jane trembled and hid her face in Elizabeth's shoulder.

The horses raced past, their hooves kicking up clods of dirt, mud spattering in the air. Most of which missed Jane entirely, and instead landed square on the head and face of Elizabeth, also spraying her gown with mud.

"Oh!" she called out.

One of the men glanced over his shoulder. His mouth opened in horror. "Whoa, hold up."

The other pulled back on his reins, an expression of irritation crossing his face, before turning himself about.

"Oh no! They're coming around!" Elizabeth considered leaping into the trees. "I'd rather die than be here for this."

"But there's no other choice, is there?" Jane always spoke sensibly, much to her consternation.

"I don't suppose there is. Come, we must stand tall." She tugged on Jane to stand with her, then straightened her shoulders, but she wasn't certain what to do with the mud sliding down her face, so she left it.

Jane moved out from behind Elizabeth, and when the men were before them, they performed their curtsys.

But Elizabeth's was noticeably shorter than Jane's. She could hardly bear to speak for her embarrassment. As it was, they weren't introduced, so she was under no obligation to do so.

Elizabeth's eyes were drawn, against her will, to the riders. One was dark, the other light, both dressed impeccably, their features striking, and their presence commanding.

She tried to shield herself with her bonnet, but she couldn't help but steal a glance. Her initial irritation with them gave way to an unsettling sensation. She felt the intensity of the darker man's gaze upon her, and it was disconcerting. She couldn't deny that he was handsome, but she was determined not to be swayed by it.

Her heartbeat quickened as his eyes continued to stay locked on her. It was as though he could see right through her, and she felt exposed. But just as she noticed him noticing her, he abruptly averted his gaze.

It was a moment that left Elizabeth with conflicting emotions. She didn't want to be attracted to a man who had little care that he had just splattered her with mud, but there was an undeniable magnetic pull she couldn't ignore. Her irritation mingled with a growing curiosity about the enigmatic dark stranger.

The first leapt off his horse and swept into a most gallant bow. "You must allow me to apologize. We were going at speeds far too fast for these roads."

Elizabeth nodded, somewhat mollified.

Jane stepped forward. "Oh please, do not trouble yourself. You surely did not see us."

The man's smile filled his face as he took in the sight of Jane, who Elizabeth would call the most beautiful woman most men ever beheld. She beamed with light inside as well as out. And this man was obviously not immune to Jane's unwitting charms.

He bowed again. "You are most gracious in your forgiveness. I do hope to make it up to you. Might we come calling? Be introduced properly?"

Jane dipped her head. "Yes, that would be lovely. We are at Longbourn."

He exchanged a pleased expression with his friend, who had yet to say a word.

Elizabeth turned the full force of her displeasure on him.

His dark eyes flashed down at her from the top of his horse, and he tipped his hat with one hand. "I do hope you are well."

"Do I look well, sir?" She lifted her chin in kind to show what must be an awfully dirty person, mud clumping off her chin and down her neck.

"You do indeed look well. I was merely asking after your injuries. Have you any?"

For a moment, she thought he showed concern, but it flashed from his face as quickly as it had come.

"We are well in that regard, thank you." She looked away. Though by far the most handsome man of any she'd laid eyes on, she would not give him an easy form of forgiveness, for he had none of his friend's easygoing manners nor his remorse.

He nodded and said nothing more. A pointed glance at his friend brought the amiable one back on his horse. The two nodded almost in unison and then continued on their way, at a walk this time.

"Well!" Elizabeth huffed. "I don't think I shall ever rid my bonnet of this stain." She removed it from her head. The dirt clod had indeed ruined her feather, but the rest looked as though nothing permanent had tainted it. Her gown might be cleansed. Their maid would not be pleased, but Elizabeth had brought home worse. The hems of her garments were often covered in mud.

"You are not so poorly off. Though your face is a sight." Jane laughed. "I cannot believe you showed it to them. You, Elizabeth, are a mind unto yourself."

"And why shouldn't I show them? Did they not cause my current state?" She replaced the bonnet. "Though I do admit that I'm not as badly presented as I feared."

Jane put a hand to her mouth. "My dear. You shall think differently when you see a looking glass. But as we both know, a little dirt never harmed a soul." She linked her hand in Elizabeth's again. "Come, let's get into the bath. For who knows when such men might come calling."

"If my getting splattered in mud leads you to fall in love with a worthy man, then I shall call it well worth the experience."

"In love, she says. I don't know the man at all." Jane blushed furiously.

"Oh, but you'd like to."

Jane laughed. "Indeed I would. If only his friend could have been half as amiable."

"Truly, I don't think he was even sorry for splattering me in mud."

"He had to have been. What man would not be?"

"Words indicating as much did not leave his mouth, and his countenance is so severe. I do find him rather prideful."

"Perhaps he is. We shall soon see, I do hope. Will they come calling, do you suppose?"

Elizabeth stepped faster. "We had best be returning home to see. And perhaps clean the drawing room of evidence of poor needlepoint."

"Oh, you are so correct."

They both stepped faster, their conversation sweet and full of laughter for the remaining walk home. Though Elizabeth had new hope for Jane, she could not shake the growing irritation with the prideful other gentleman. How could he not even apologize? His friend had shown him a fine example to follow and yet he remained on his horse and, after a brief asking after her well-being, had ridden off.

Surely he could not be a man worthy of consideration. And he seemed far from being willing to participate in a harmless flirtation, which might have been an option for even a prideful man if he was as handsome as that one had been. Lizzy knew Jane would be mortified at her thoughts, but she had them nonetheless.

Alas, Elizabeth was in the same single state as she ever had been. But Jane, on the other hand. Perhaps things were about to change for her dear Jane.

Chapter Two

A day, then another, and even a week passed with no word from the gentlemen. Elizabeth was about ready to burn their memory in a grand effigy with every despondent look from Jane.

Surely the one pleasing man would make good on his word, unless the lofty one convinced him otherwise. Elizabeth's brain conjured up all sorts of scenarios that vilified the darker man, while the lighter man became the hero of his own tragedy, kept from his love by a villainous traitor.

The two sisters sat at breakfast, Jane merely toying with her biscuit and Elizabeth not interested in her tea. After too many moments of despondency, Jane sat forward. "We are wasting our lives, sitting here, hoping for a man to show up who can rescue us all from ruin."

Elizabeth swallowed, then tilted her head. "Excuse me?" Her mind reeled at Jane's honesty. "Usually I'm the one to be more . . . blunt." She smiled, then reached for Jane's hand.

"But I see you've been correct all along. We must make a life for ourselves. We must find marriage, find love . . . ourselves."

Elizabeth nodded slowly, eyeing her sister. "What happened to you in your sleep?"

Jane's mouth tugged in a smile, and then she laughed. "Nothing. I just realized the futility of meeting a handsome man—an amiable, smiling, kind, handsome man—and then simply sitting here while we hope he will call."

Elizabeth lifted her teacup in salute.

"And I think there is more we can do. Who is he? Why is he here? Surely the Lucases have some sort of gossip about him." She slumped back in her seat. "Perhaps he is already gone."

Not wanting to stifle this new active side of her typically passive sister, Elizabeth was quick to respond. "What do you propose we do? Shall we go into town, ask around? Perhaps hope to see them?"

Jane nodded, then stood. "Yes. And I shall wear my most fetching bonnet."

Elizabeth joined her. "Good, then. I'll dress as well."

She hurried off to the same bedchamber, calling for Hill.

Partway through their ministrations, Jane being extra careful with every detail of her presentation, Elizabeth rested a hand on her arm. "Jane. You are lovely and desirable just the way you are. Be yourself. That's all that is needed."

She shook her head. "Myself, these many minutes of preparation, and an active plan to be and do the things that would encourage marriage. That is what is needed."

Elizabeth felt that feather of discomfort when things weren't exactly as they should be, but she said nothing, and soon she and Jane were out the door, walking at a brisk pace toward town.

Jane wrapped her shawl tighter across her shoulders. "Surely someone knows something about these gentlemen. If not the Lucases, then perhaps the regiment. Your Wickham might very well have some inkling."

"We don't even know their names. Did you like him that much?"

Jane's face wrinkled in a flash of pain, and she looked away. "I cannot explain the intensity of my feelings except that he seemed to be everything that is good."

"But you hardly spoke three words. And he splattered mud all over us."

"His apology was so gallant and immediate. I knew right away that a man who could admit wrong so quickly would be lovely to live with." Her face burned bright red. "I realize this is all rather untoward."

Elizabeth linked their arms. "I don't think it so untoward. Perhaps a bit . . . abrupt, speaking of living with someone. But I cannot disagree with your assessment. He seemed to recover quickly from a rather large faux pas."

"Was it so very large?"

When Elizabeth turned disbelieving eyes her direction, Jane laughed. "Yes, I suppose particularly to you, who received the brunt of it, they were rather careless and reckless."

She nodded. "But we shall forgive the more amiable of the two."

"And not his friend?" Jane searched her face. "He, too, was quite handsome."

"But not handsome enough to tempt me, not when he could not descend from his horse to apologize." She frowned. "I'm sure at this point it is he who has discouraged a visit, he who would make things difficult."

Jane shook her head. "I'm not certain how you can know such a thing, really."

"No more than you can know the fairer of the two is amiable and worthy of such interest from my dear and nearly perfect Jane."

She stepped closer. "Too true. Now that we are speaking sense, I realize what a foolish creature I must seem." She stopped. "Shall we return home? I do not wish to be chasing a man about the place."

Elizabeth shook her head. "No, let's go on. A walk is always good for the soul, and who knows what we may learn in town."

Jane nudged her. “Perhaps my mention of the militia sparked some interest?”

She laughed. “Only a little. I do find Wickham adorable in his way. Handsome, certainly. But we both know he is nothing more than a flirtation. How could he be anything but?”

“The way you speak of flirtations, Lizzy, you’re scandalous. I don’t know if I should be ashamed of you or not.” Jane’s face was again pink.

“Please don’t feel anything but pleased for me. I know what I’m about. I’ve done nothing scandalous.” She squeezed her sister’s arm. “You know me better than that.”

Jane did not look convinced. But they walked on, speaking of lighter, more pleasant things. This time of year was a glorious season to be out and about as long as it wasn’t raining. The buds were emerging. The flowers from last spring were peeking the barest touch of color from the earth. And the air smelt of rain and wet earth and greenery. Lizzy, in truth, loved everything about spring.

Their last approach into Meryton found them cutting through the center of a large meadow. The path was well worn and kept the grasses away so that their ankles were not tickled by the tall waving blades, which seemed to stretch for miles in every direction. The soft breeze tickled the tops of the grasses, creating waves of movement all around them. Elizabeth stopped and held out her arms. “When we stand right here, I feel as though we are the center of something beautiful." She lifted her face to the sun. "And I get far too many freckles."

Jane laughed. "Let me try it." She held her arms out and slowly spun.

The sound of horses' hooves brought a gasp from Jane.

They both turned toward two riders making their way across the meadow. Jane clutched Elizabeth's arm. "Is it them?"

Lizzy lifted a hand and squinted against the sun. "Could be." She pried Jane's fingers off her forearm. "But we must behave as though we have not come searching for them."

"Oh yes, you're correct." She took two steps toward town and then turned back. "But do we just stand here?"

"I think that would be acceptable." Lizzy nodded. "Or perhaps we keep walking to town?" They began a careful staged walk on the path.

The sounds of horses galloping drew nearer.

"Surely they would not just race on by as they did before," Elizabeth muttered.

"Do we even know it is them?"

"We do not."

"Perhaps we should stop walking and look again?"

"Yes, you are correct." She turned again toward the horses, who were now close enough that Elizabeth recognized at once the tall, arrogant form of the darker-haired man.

Jane sucked in a breath beside her. "It is him."

"And now we wait. For we've looked silly enough starting and stopping." She freed herself from Jane's arm grip and clasped her hands behind her back, her chin high.

"They are still going at such a fast pace." Jane inched closer to Lizzy. "What if they don't stop?"

"Then they are both as reprehensible as I believe the darker one to be."

But in the next moment, both horses eased off their pace and the men moved forward at a walk, the golden hair of the one peeking out from beneath his hat in the sun. He dipped his head, but they were too far as yet for them to communicate anything more.

Jane lifted her hand in greeting. Lizzy did nothing, but she felt the stare of the dark-haired one as though he saw right through her. Surely it was her imagination. She guessed he hardly noticed her, so far beneath his attention she must be. But there was that unmistakable sensation that someone was watching, specifically him, and to her surprise, it was not unpleasant.

Chapter Three

Fitzwilliam Darcy tried not to notice the beautiful Miss Elizabeth Bennet. But with her arms out and her face turned up into the sun, he found himself enchanted.

So enchanted that he looked away and frowned. He'd just as soon have ridden on the opposite side of the meadow to flee their presence, but naturally, Bingley had adjusted their direction and headed immediately toward Miss Jane Bennet. The man was as besotted as any young school boy who'd never seen a beautiful woman before.

The women were clearly waiting for them. So he took the time of his approach to allow himself the luxury of studying Miss Elizabeth. She stood proudly, sensibly, trying to act unaffected by him. Perhaps she was truly unaffected. He'd learned early on to not give women the slightest provocation, no feather of inclination on his part to pursue. Such mistaken overtures were only grievous to all involved. Darcy was not free to pursue any woman, not at the moment. Perhaps one day. But unless the woman was perfectly clear of his intentions, which were to not become entangled, then he must be the most aloof he could.

Elizabeth's hair shone in the sun.

And such a woman would be hard to resist if the day came when he *were* actually free. Her nose was pert—much like her personality, if he were to guess. He allowed himself a small smile. She looked to be intelligent. And she was not simpering, bold enough to be rightfully irritated with him for staying aloft on his horse on their previous encounter.

His smile grew. She was undoubtedly the kind of woman who would stand up to his ideas, challenge his intellect, perhaps even make him laugh.

"They are lovely, aren't they?" Bingley grinned into his face. Drat, the man had seen his smile.

"As lovely as any two creatures I've seen, but take care, Bingley, we don't know much beyond the fact that their father is a local landowner."

"What more do I need to know with a face such as hers?" Bingley placed a hand at his chest.

All Darcy could do was laugh at his friend. "You, sir, are a hopeless romantic."

"And you, a hopeless cynic."

He nodded. "'Tis true."

"But I suppose I would be as well if I were in your shoes.

Come, Darcy, enjoy the company of these fine women. You deserve it as much as the next gentleman." Bingley lifted his chin in Miss Elizabeth's direction. "And she doesn't look like the type to misconstrue a bit of friendliness."

Darcy considered him, and in that moment, Miss Elizabeth laughed at something her sister said, and her whole face broke into a ray of such loveliness, he caught his breath. "Perhaps you're correct . . ."

Bingley's laugh hardly registered with Darcy as they finished their approach. Perhaps just for a week, he could enjoy her company—not even a flirtation, but a friendship. Where both parties were attractive, and he enjoyed the lady's company.

Her smiling face turned to him, her lips wide and welcoming. Perhaps something a bit more than friendship . . . And then her countenance changed, and she lost a measure of her sparkle. He almost burst out laughing as she managed to frown in his direction. Oh, she was a delight.

She and Miss Jane curtsied together.

He leapt off his horse and joined Bingley in a smart bow, determined to see the light in her face return. Perhaps one day she would laugh in his direction like she'd just done to Miss Jane.

He rose from his bow. "It is good to see you ladies on a fine walk this morning." His smile was large and welcoming. He couldn't resist, even though he knew she might misconstrue his intentions.

Miss Elizabeth started for a moment but then smiled, only demurely, in return. "We didn't know you were still in town."

Bingley erupted in a string of exclamations and profuse explanations as to why they were only just now coming calling. "We were just on our way to see you in fact, right now." He paused, his eyes widening in hope.

Darcy needed to save him from himself. He opened his mouth to temper his friend's statements, but Miss Jane turned a most attractive pink and stepped closer. "You are too good, sir. We are well, and I am only too glad to hear you were indeed coming to call." She looked away in a manner most fetching, and Darcy knew if his friend was not smitten before, he most certainly was now. "I cannot tell you how many times I've stared down the lane, wondering at your arrival."

A small noise came from Miss Elizabeth, but when Darcy directed his attention back to her, her face was blank. Did she groan? Was she equally aghast at their friends' overly floral effusions? He studied her in a new light and then attempted a bit of humor.

"I, for one, am not as effusive, but I do think this will save us the ride." He almost grinned, but then Miss Elizabeth stiffened.

"You needn't have bothered," she said.

"But here we are." He indicated their companions, who were now deep in quiet conversation.

She stood taller. "Well, then. I shall be more than pleased to find my own company as we all walk back from town."

"Or perhaps we could venture back into town together. I hear there is a rather remarkable bakery?" He dipped his head, eyes up, waiting.

She studied him a moment more, glanced at her sister, who seemed to have forgotten anyone but Bingley existed in the world, and then nodded. "The bakery does have a delightful custard I've been eyeing."

"Excellent. I haven't had a good custard in ages. Our town baker outside my estate in Pemberley makes the best custards."

"Does he? We shall have to see if ours rival the shades of Pemberley, then, shan't we?"

He bowed. "Miss Elizabeth. Miss Jane. Shall we be off, then?"

Her soft intake of breath made him smile. "Yes, I have discovered your names." He couldn't resist a bit of enjoyment about their cleverness.

"And are we not to know yours?" Her one eyebrow rose a little higher than the other.

He considered her and then looked away. "I think not yet."

When her mouth dropped open, he tipped his head back and laughed. "Come now. You might enjoy a bit of a mystery."

She grumbled to herself a moment, but dipped her head in acquiescence, which he assumed would be temporary. They fell in step, one couple in front of the other, the horses on long leads, Miss Elizabeth and Darcy taking up the rear. His horse, Samson, walked at his side.

Miss Jane's giggle carried to them as they walked along.

Darcy found no need for talking simply for talking's sake, but he was intrigued by this woman at his side. And he wondered what would happen if he took Bingley's advice for a change and befriended her.

"Tell me, Miss Elizabeth, how do you like living so close to Meryton?"

She leaned her heat a bit closer to him. "I like it very much. We have friends nearby and the shops and dances bring much diversion." She smiled. "As well as the militia that is often stationed nearby. There are always many activities meant to create diversion and recreation for them."

He nodded. "And do you aspire to marrying a man of uniform?"

Her eyes widening a hint should have warned him of what was coming.

"Who do you aspire to marry?" she asked.

"Pardon me?"

"You certainly feel comfortable inquiring after my personal affairs on so short an acquaintance. I thought I would as well."

"Since you have not as yet answered me, I feel no

responsibility to divulge anything about my future marriage."

"Excellent. Then we are in agreement." She turned her face from him for a moment, then jerked her head back. "Are you engaged to be married?"

He choked. "No. I'm not."

She nodded again. "Good, then."

Chapter Four

Lizzy didn't know what to make of this new side to the dark villain of her stories. What was she even to call him? She stopped. "Sir."

"Yes?" His eyebrow quirked with a hint of amusement.

"I still do not know what to call you. And though you glean a wicked enjoyment in the fact, shall we now be introduced?"

"We shall, yes, we should. These sorts of situations are quite untoward, aren't they? We can't very well be walking all the way to Meryton not knowing to whom we are speaking."

"Precisely."

"But on the other hand, we've no one to introduce us." He smiled, and the full force of his happiness was difficult to resist, but Lizzy rallied.

"We are at a greater disadvantage here, surely. You can

inquire anywhere in town to know much about us. Already you are calling us by name. You, on the other hand, are entirely unknown."

"Too true." His eyebrow wiggled.

"Are you enjoying your advantage, then?"

"I am, to be honest."

After a moment or two of silence, she huffed. "So you will not tell who you are? You hail from Pemberley, you say? Where is your estate?"

"I'm quite proud of it, actually. We reside in the lake country, Derbyshire."

"Oh lovely. And have you relatives here in town?"

"I do not."

"So the nature of your visit is . . ." She waited, her hands out.

"I am here as a support to my friend." He began walking again, and with his legs long as they were, Lizzy had to hurry to keep up. And when she caught sight of his expression, she had to laugh at the smirk that remained.

"And you really won't tell me who you are?"

"We will just have to wait to be introduced, I suppose. It doesn't matter, really. Nothing could come of two strangers meeting in a field."

She looked on ahead at two people very obviously connecting, but she said nothing. Even if this strange new villain in her life turned out to be more interesting than she previously imagined, she already saw him behave in a despicable manner, knew he was capable of villainy, and she might not forgive such a thing.

"Though a meeting in a field might not lead to a lasting commitment, it might provide some fun diversion." One eyebrow rose just a hair above the other, and his expression took on such a look of daring, she almost laughed out loud.

"Just what are you saying?"

"Nothing at all, unless you want me to be." This time his expression revealed nothing, and Lizzy didn't quite know what to make of him. But if he was suggesting a possible flirtation, like she thought he might be, then she just might be interested. Was she not just talking about that very thing this very day? Did she not long for some companionship, a little adventure, something different from her everyday? That, she did.

And in this regard, he might be handsome enough to tempt her after all. Her face heated. She knew she was turning a bright pink.

"What's this? Are you blushing?" He stopped their walking again. "So you're interested?"

Jane was far away, so she couldn't hear what Lizzy was saying. Did she dare?

This new stranger with all his mysterious ways had eyes the color of coal. His smile started small and grew slowly across his face, revealing a row of white teeth. Oh, he was handsome indeed.

She grinned in response.

"Might I presume you mean yes, then?"

"You might." She hardly believed her own words. "Your offer comes at the precise right moment, as I have nothing else to do and no one else to misbehave with."

"Misbehave?" He laughed. "What if I thought to misbehave in exactly the correct way? Rest assured, your reputation is safe with me. I simply wish to know a woman, converse with a woman, perhaps hold a woman's hand without any of the typical entanglements."

She nodded. "That is precisely what I have been wishing for. But sir, I cannot create a scandal. No seeming attachments here followed by your disappearance. We must be careful that no one suspects a growing interest or an intent to marry. That could ruin me as much as anything."

"Understood. We shall be careful indeed. I shall be in the area for a time." He lifted his chin in Jane's direction. "And perhaps the two of them will give us excuse and reason enough to be together."

Jane and this new stranger's heads were bent together in conversation. They had not ceased enjoying each other for the entirety of their walk.

Lizzy returned his mischievous grin with one of her own. "Perfect. Now, to get an introduction." She shook her head. "You are mysterious."

"And you will have your introduction soon enough."

She stepped closer and placed her hand on his arm. "So, tell me Mr. Nonesuch, what do you like to do to relax?"

"To relax?"

"Yes. I'm going to assume you are a busy man, that you concern yourself over others, and that the moments for you to relax are few. What do you do in those moments?"

His eyes flashed with trouble, but then they cleared. "That is an astute observation. Do I relax? I suppose I travel with friends in need of direction, and while I am away, I relax."

"Like now?"

"Precisely now. I am relaxing this moment."

"I'm unaccountably proud of that."

He eyed her a moment, and then lifted his chin and laughed to the heavens. "Are you?"

"Yes, I am."

"As you should be. There are not many who have seen me relax, almost none who have been the cause of it."

She squeezed his arm. "Are you that troubled usually?"

"Perhaps, or the better word might be responsible? I have a great deal to manage."

She nodded. What manner of man was this? Perhaps a lord? She guessed he managed a large estate. Or if it wasn't large, it felt so to him. "Then I'm pleased we have made our arrangement. I suspect it will do us both a bit of good."

"I suspect you are correct." He raised a hand toward Jane. "Now what shall we do about our friends there?"

They were still speaking as intimately as ever.

"I don't know that anything needs to be done. What if they are happy?"

"Is there any reason my friend would be making a poor attachment there?"

She stiffened.

He held up a hand. "I can tell your sister is as lovely as any woman ever could be—besides yourself. I simply am asking if she, too, is prone to harmless flirtations?"

"No, she's as sincere a person as there ever was."

"So is my friend." He turned back to her. "And now, my turn to ask a question."

"Are we taking turns?"

"We are now, I think." He grinned. "Tell me the most daring thing you've ever done."

This flirtation with a stranger was by far the most daring thing Lizzy had ever done. But she wasn't about to admit such a thing. "I am not certain what to admit. The most daring, you say?" She tapped a finger on her mouth. "I'd have to say, the day I told Mama I would not be marrying Mr. Collins."

His eyes widened. "Oh, stumbled on a gold mine. Do tell me about the loathed Mr. Collins."

She drooped her shoulders a bit.

"Oh dear, no. Not if it dampens your spirits. We can talk of something else."

"It is a rather diverting tale, truth be told. I am struggling to know where to begin."

"Skip to the interesting parts."

"I shall also attempt not to reveal more about my identity as well. Since we are being so embarrassingly proper as to await introductions." She sighed.

"Rather diverting, is it not?"

"Not at all. Now, on to the interesting bits. A distant cousin appeared on our doorstep, offering to marry one of us off."

"Just like that? And did he expect you would be accepting of such an offer? How many of you was he proposing to at once?"

She laughed. "Five."

"Goodness. He offered his hand to one of you five? And your mother suggested you?"

"I . . . think so? I'm not entirely certain, as most men are at first drawn to Jane."

"I cannot account for that."

"You cannot?" She studied him. "You were not first drawn to Jane?"

"I wasn't. You were the first I noticed, and I have not been intrigued by anything in your sister that would cause my attention to linger there." He shrugged. "You have a dark interest that captured me immediately."

She blushed. There was nothing for it. "You are quite gifted with your words, sir."

"I suspect the same of you. What was the first thing you noticed about me?"

"Before or after your frown?"

"Either. Before. Tell me what you thought of me, frown and all."

She wasn't certain how to answer that. She was meant to be flirting, not insulting. The truth was very telling, though. Did she wish to admit her immediate attraction? She decided she would. He could take her thoughts however he liked. "I thought you the same. Dark, intriguing, tempting." She bit her tongue, shocked at her own daring.

"But?" His expression was teasing. There was a bit of the devil in him, she decided.

"But . . . you didn't get off your horse, nor apologize. And I had mud sliding down my face." She stopped and crossed her arms. "There."

"I have never seen a more captivating mud-clad woman I swear it." He held a hand on his heart. "If I was free, I'd have fallen in love straightaway." His eyebrow wiggled, just a hair, and she knew more of that devil was coming out.

"I don't even want to believe you at this point." She returned her hand to his arm. "But your words are pretty, so I'll let the whole thing go in favor of our fun conversation."

His eyes were on her, but she refused to turn to him again.

"I know I owe you an apology." His voice was soft, sincere. His eyes were full of remorse. "You did not deserve my treatment. I hold myself aloof. I don't engage with others. It was unfair and unkind."

She studied him, her heart irrevocably touched by his sincerity. "Thank you," she murmured.

He swooped into a grand bow and then rose with hopeful eyes. "That was not sufficient." He held a hand to his heart. "Oh, my dear lady. I was irreparably rude. Would you allow me to take this moment to most grandly, and with great flourish, apologize?" He dipped in another very low, very gallant bow, twirling his hand at the end of it as though bowing at St. James.

She considered him. He hadn't explained himself. But he was apologizing in the best manner a man could. So she nodded. "Yes, I accept your apology. And I know that perhaps next time, you will not only descend your lofty horse, but will offer a handkerchief?"

He nodded. "I'll offer one now. A token?" He held it out with a grin.

"Thank you. I'll take it." She tucked it carefully into her reticule, and then they continued walking.

"I feel we know each other so much better now, don't you?" He tucked her hand into the crook of his arm. "I'm going to enjoy our friendship immensely." He pointed to a bit of flowers peeking out of the ground. "Are those crocuses?"

Grasping on to a lighter conversation, she hurried to answer. "They are. And this is almost the time for them to start appearing. Those are early." They paused their walk for a moment. The blue tips made her smile. "Hardy things, aren't they? The first to appear, coming even when the weather isn't the most inviting, and lasting until the others can survive."

"How poetic."

"I didn't know I had it in me. I've been known to say that there is nothing like bad poetry to drive away feelings of romance."

"Surely not. How many have fallen while reading Shakespeare's ballads? Or dare I say, Byron?" His mock horror-filled face made her laugh again.

Elizabeth dipper her head in acknowledgement of Shakespeare. "I will always defer to the Bard. He is the master of all poems. But Byron? Come now. Who would want to attempt such a thing as a kiss after reading his weak attempts?"

"Oh, she dares critique the master of our day. How many would faint straightaway at your words?"

"I care not to know, nor would I countenance Byron to encourage romantic feelings."

"I am taking note. No Byron. But Shakespeare would be welcome?" His eyes filled with hope, and she was, for a moment, lost in them. His boyish charm she would have never suspected, his cheerful countenance, the hope of impressing her. She was in danger of losing sight of the friendship aspect of their agreement.

She cleared her throat as if to shake the rising attraction.

"I would most welcome Shakespeare. And if you know that, you might guess at some others as well."

He smiled, his lips suddenly something of interest to her.

"And wilt thou have me fashion into speech
The love I bear thee, finding words enough,
And hold the torch out, while the winds are rough,
Between our faces, to cast light on each?"

Lizzy smiled. "Elizabeth Browning."

"The very one. By way of reference, would she do?"

"Yes, she would do very nicely." Her mind spun. Her knees shook beneath her skirts. Her hands were kept still by the sheer force of her will.

She walked at his side, listening to him point out this or that lovely thing about her home, about one of her most traversed walks, and she could not help herself. She fell half in love with the man.

Not really, of course, but she would have liked to. Without knowing a thing about him, she knew so much more than she did about most other men. The more she discovered, the more she admired. And that was a refreshing thing indeed.

Chapter Five

B*e careful, Darcy,* he told himself again and again that evening as he readied for the assembly dance in Meryton. No need to become attached to a woman who would surely never be his. But nothing wrong with dressing his best for the assembly. He was certain Miss Elizabeth Bennet would be present, with her sister. And it was there he would be revealed—his name, his identity, and therefore his yearly income. He had yet to meet a woman who could resist his wealth. But perhaps Elizabeth would be the rare woman who could simply continue their friendship without the distraction of trying to secure his estate and money.

What would she do? Would she begin to fawn over him? Attempt to win his fortune? Time would tell. But he certainly hoped he'd not lose his new friend.

She'd become that. A friendship had found its way into

their conversation, a delightfully challenging and intelligent sort of friendship, one he'd be loath to lose. At least so early on. Of course he could not be her friend for the rest of his life, but for this spring and summer while Bingley moved in to the neighborhood? Certainly.

Once his valet finished preparing him for the assembly, Darcy studied his appearance in the mirror, eyeing his cravat. "Something is different. What is it?" he asked.

"I tried a new knot. I believe it suits you."

Darcy turned this way and that so he might get a good look at it. Then he nodded. "I believe you are correct. It does suit me." Would Miss Elizabeth notice such a thing? Now instead of dreading all that a country assembly might bring, he was in a hurry to again see Miss Elizabeth to learn if she was the type of woman to notice a man's cravat. How perfectly enjoyable to have a secret friend.

It was a bit unfair that he knew her identity. But he couldn't be entertaining flirtations with just anyone. And her family was one of the most respected in the county.

He and Bingley pulled in front of the assembly rooms in Meryton. "I believe we are going to have a good time of it, don't you?" Bingley's smile was larger than usual, which was saying something.

"You are correct. And might I point out without offending you that it shall be much merrier without your sisters?"

"Too true, old friend. You know they arrive in a fortnight."

"I do, yes. Until then, we shall have to make the most of our time without their ever-present eyes and overly engaged curiosity."

Bingley took on a look of embarrassed apology. "Caroline will not accept that your future is attached elsewhere. I have tried to explain."

"I know it. Women find the prospect of Pemberley and all that the estate gifts our family difficult to resist. Not that your sister is mercenary, just that she is much like every other lady of the ton. In some ways, my promise of an impending engagement to someone else gifts me with the shield of protection against those who would attempt to win my heart insincerely."

"And how is Miss Anne?"

Darcy rubbed his forehead. "I cannot tell. I presume she is as well as ever, which is only mildly healthy. Lady Catherine is good to keep me informed of her welfare. And remind me of my duties."

"Does the ever-dutiful Darcy have a sudden disinclination?"

"What makes you say that?"

"Just your tone. For the first time in my years of knowing you, you are speaking of your possible nuptials as though they are tiring."

"I suppose they are always tiresome. Would they not be to you?"

Bingley shook his head. "I don't know. I hope that one day, thoughts of my nuptials will bring me the greatest happiness." He opened up the carriage door before the footmen could approach. "Now come, man. There are two beautiful women who must receive an introduction so that I might dance with one."

Darcy laughed, following his friend out of the carriage.

And was immediately crowded about by hordes of people.

The smells filling the night air were perhaps not unbearable were they isolated, but the combination of sweat, perfumed waters, foul breath, old cheese, thick waste mixed in the mud at their feet, and that of the animals driving carriages assaulted Darcy's senses. He stopped just short of placing a handkerchief at his nose. He turned to his footman. "Get us out of this."

"Yes, Mr. Darcy."

Someone nearby gasped and then whispered to the woman at her right, who then continued spreading whispers of his name to the nearby vicinity.

Which in some ways aided his servants in clearing a place in the crowd and opening up a space for them to walk to the front door. "Insufferable," he muttered under his breath.

But Bingley, of course, heard. "Oh, Darcy. Tonight is a

good opportunity for you to let go of some of these sensibilities. See, your servant has us inside and no worse for the wear."

Darcy did not answer. For a moment only, he gazed on the pleased, happy smiles in the room with distress. How could he meet such expectations from others when he barely arrived in the door without turning back? Then he saw how they interacted with one another and his distress turned to a slight yearning. If only he could enjoy such closeness with others. But the longing passed as the sense of entrapment enclosed on him. His quick perusal of the room told him this would be an evening to be endured only. Beads of sweat cooled his forehead, but he needed to find an elevated place with some air around him. And now.

He resisted tugging at his cravat and instead lifted his chin. "Go find your woman with her pretty smiles. She will keep you well and truly distracted. Leave me to my grumblings." He waved off his friend.

But Bingley stood closer. "I'll not have you moping about. Make an attempt at enjoyment. My lady is the most beautiful creature I've ever laid eyes on, true. But her sister is her equal in wit and beauty."

"She is tolerable I suppose, but not handsome enough to tempt me. No. Off with you. Pester me no further."

Once Bingley had turned his back, Darcy smiled to himself. The first step in his and Miss Elizabeth's secret was to ensure that even his closest friend did not suspect. Surely

Bingley would hint at a closeness between him and Elizabeth and give away their secret forthwith if he suspected an attachment of any kind.

The crowd parted somewhat to let him pass. He'd found just the right place to wait out the evening: an elevated spot near the instruments just off the lit areas on the dance floor. He walked as quickly as he was able and counted breaths until he arrived. Perhaps here he would be allowed a moment to control his pounding heart. He'd never done well with crowds. Tight spaces exacerbated everything.

When he at last stood a bit apart, he hid shaking hands. Years of reprimands from his father did nothing to ease his discomfort. He'd learned long ago he couldn't simply wish the panicked feeling away. He didn't like crowds. He didn't like tight spaces. And that was that. A few moments of controlled breathing and he might conquer the angst without outside air and clean spaces.

And then suddenly Miss Elizabeth was standing in front of him, arms crossed, with a rather large scowl. He'd never seen anyone so stunning. Fire burst from her eyes and her cheeks flamed red. She was breathtaking when angry, though he had to also admit, fearsome. He attempted to ignore her—they had not been introduced, after all—but she moved to stand directly in his line of sight and very, very close indeed.

"What are you doing?" he hissed, looking over the top of her head.

"Not handsome enough to tempt you?" She huffed. "What was that?"

His eyes flit to hers. "You heard that?"

"As did half the room. I'm getting pity stares. Pity. Stares. Mr. Darcy. Yes, I know who you are. You will ask me to dance this instant to correct the room in their thinking that I am so far beneath you."

"And our introduction?"

She waved her hand in the air. "We will pretend it has happened." She shifted her weight onto her other hip, arms still crossed, waiting.

He knew it was the wrong moment, but the sound just bubbled out of him, of its own accord. A laugh as deep and delicious as he'd had in many months. "Oh, my dear Miss Elizabeth. I'm afraid we've found ourselves in a bit of a quandary."

"And why is that?" Her mouth twitched, her eyes showing a brilliant sparkle that proved she would have liked to laugh as well. He found that almost as delicious as his own laugh.

"Because I do not dance at assemblies such as this. If I go out on the floor with you, I shall have to repeat the practice with another, else we shall have no harmless flirtation at all. In fact, we can no longer converse if you do not wish for rumors to fly of the other variety. I insulted you to my friend so that he would not guess our intentions."

Her eyes widened and she stepped back to give them a more appropriate distance. "I see."

"You also see the trouble I'm having."

"But you must see my trouble. I'll not have them thinking you are slighting me." She stood taller, and though her height did not even come close to matching his, he admired her effort.

"Surely you won't stand for such a thing."

She narrowed her eyes.

"And even now if you wish, I will act as though I'm petitioning for a dance." He bowed over her hand, and placed a kiss on the back. Her mouth dropped open and she fell into a deep curtsy.

"Now you step back, shake your head, and I shall look as disappointed as I'm able."

She considered him a moment and then shook her head. "No." Her arms relaxed, her expression softened, and she reached out her hand. "Will you dance with me?"

He had no choice. A gentleman would never refuse. It didn't matter that a lady would never ask. She had asked. And he now must consent. But what they were going to do about their flirtation would need to be settled later. He could enjoy this dance. And then suffer at the hands of many others the night through. Perhaps Miss Elizabeth would consent to dance more than just the one.

Chapter Six

Elizabeth wished she could say she didn't know what came over her. But she knew. Mr. Darcy had captured her attention, and she was not able to resist. And why should she? Why could she not dance with the most eligible man in the room? Why could she not flirt with him, be enamored with him? He'd said himself that he was not free to pursue a woman. So be it. She was not pursing him either. But she was highly interested in spending time with him, and of course she would be. He was the most interesting thing to happen to her, to Meryton, in the history of their village.

She kept her hand out, knowing he would not refuse her, knowing they would get a dance. Music for the longest country reel began, and her smile grew. "Come, Mr. Darcy. I dare say you will survive this country dance."

He stepped nearer, so near she could smell the musky

spices of his scent. His eyes had darkened, turned as serious as she'd ever seen them. "You have captured me, heart and soul, woman, and I dare say I shall not survive the longest country reel of all time with a woman I am attempting to pretend doesn't affect me, but I could not refuse such a request." He dipped his head. "Nor do I wish to do so. We will weather the repercussions later. Might I have the second as well?" His breath tickled her neck as he leaned ever closer to hear her response. "I cannot abide one dance only."

Her throat dried, her lips suddenly parted. She could refuse him nothing. "I no longer even care if it is wise. You may. A third, if you wish."

"Then come, I shall see only you." He led her out to the dance floor with head high, shoulders back, a slight smile on his face. As she turned to face him, the realization of whom she was standing with resting upon her, she felt her confidence waver. Mr. Darcy was by far the most wealthy of her acquaintance. His aunt was noble. His estate one of the most renowned in the area. He was the most sought-after hand in marriage that England had to offer at the moment even though he did not have a title. And he stood with her, one of five daughters, with no real marriage prospects, with no real dowry, with nothing to offer such a man. She lowered her gaze.

"What's this?" Darcy's tone was clipped.

She jerked her gaze up to his, surprised at his tone.

"Have I intimidated the great Elizabeth Bennet?"

She raised her eyebrows.

"Yes, I know who you are. The most sought-after woman in all of Hartfordshire? The woman who took on the most intimidating acquaintance in the room, who confidently commanded my respect?" He raised an eyebrow. "Are you now at a loss?"

She felt the itchy rising tide of ire fill her. "Mr. Darcy."

"Yes, Miss Elizabeth?"

"I am never at a loss."

His eyebrows rose together with a challenge, as if to say, "Prove it."

And so she lifted her chin. He was a handsome man indeed. But of all the women here, she was his equal in at least something. And he wished to spend time with her, wished to be free to do so. And something inside suspected that if he were truly free, he might even think about pursuing her with sincerity. Would he really?

His attention was fully and completely captured.

Perhaps he would.

As the dance began, she stepped forward to curtsy, watching him as she lowered herself and then stood. His bow was with eyes only for her. Then they circled one another.

If anyone else noticed or talked about her great coup in gaining the first set with such a man, she did not notice or even care. She and Mr. Darcy lifted their feet, danced, moved with and around the others, but she saw nothing and no one but her partner. She heard nothing but the music. With every touch, she felt a caress, with every step, she felt his nearness. He was her all, her everything, her sun, drawing in a never-ending orbit. She'd never felt anything so powerful, not even her pull to the Earth.

The set finished with them saying nothing at all to one another, but with Elizabeth knowing it was the most intimate dance of her experience.

He lifted her hand to his lips. "Thank you." As his mouth pressed to the back of her glove, she cursed that slip of material, thin though it was, cursed its barrier shielding her skin, and then blushed furiously.

"Your countenance gives you away marvelously." His mouth wiggled in a wicked grin.

"Oh stop. You don't know what I'm blushing about. Perhaps I noticed a long-time flirtation across the room, and I cannot wait to be in his presence."

He growled. "You have not."

She lifted a shoulder. "Perhaps. Or you might never know."

He nodded to the musicians, and the three count to a waltz began. With a flourish, he bowed. "And now our next set?"

Several women in the room gasped, but Elizabeth did not look to see who was appalled by the introduction of the waltz to their community. She knew it was danced in London, knew the prince approved it and therefore they all could. But Prinny was not known for his great propriety. Luckily, she and Jane had practiced together. She stepped closer to Mr. Darcy, and he moved closer still. With a hand at her back, she felt immediately in his embrace.

And her cheeks again warmed.

"And that blush?"

She could only nod. "What can I say?"

"No words are needed."

And she'd never felt a more true sentiment. Words were not necessary.

He held her close and led them both magnificently. Many had cleared the floor, which gave them room to spin and twirl and use more of the space. Something about his control of the situation, the power in his arms, his nearness, made her want to lean in, to stand closer, to be lifted straight into his arms and carried away. They floated as if in the clouds, and she thought she could have continued thus for the rest of the evening. He leaned and she followed; he pressed into her back, she moved. He pulled her closer and she acquiesced. In truth, she would have done anything he asked, gone anywhere he led. For that moment, she was his, and it was the most glorious feeling in the world.

And then it ended.

And before Mr. Darcy could even make his bows, George Wickham was at her side with his hand outstretched.

Chapter Seven

"Might I have the next set, Miss Elizabeth?" His wicked drawl, his lazy expression, his strong arms that used to capture her intrigue did little for her when compared to the powerful man still standing as close as he had, as though they were about to waltz. She hesitated, loathe to remove her hand from her current partner's. But the moment grew. She faltered and then glanced up into Mr. Darcy's face.

But he was not looking at her. He and Mr. Wickham were in a duel of sorts, by expression only. Their eyes bore into each other. Mr. Darcy's stance stiffened. He pressed his lips together. But he said nothing.

After a moment, Mr. Wickham shrugged. "Come, Darcy, you've monopolized the most beautiful woman in the room long enough. Release your conquest."

Elizabeth bristled. "Conquest indeed." She frowned.

With a quick glance in her direction, Mr. Darcy released her hand as though he'd been singed. Then he bowed curtly to her, turned, and walked through the room, out the door, and into the night.

Elizabeth breathed out. "Goodness."

"Yes, he has that effect, I hear. Leaves broken hearts everywhere he goes."

She lifted her gaze to him. "That, I can well believe. And you, Mr. Wickham, how many hearts have you left in your wake?"

He did not answer her directly for a moment, but led her to their place for another reel. "I am most certain I shall not be taking any piece of your heart with me. More's the pity. But perhaps I've gained something no one else has?" His eyes challenged her, his comment voicing their hidden flirtations, their conversations when no one would see. She'd been most appropriate, but he made it sound as though they'd been truly naughty.

"You forget yourself," she hissed.

"Do I? Or are you hoping that Mr. Darcy will continue where I left off?" His words, whispered in her ear as he passed, singed her.

"Stop, at once."

"How can you abide such a man?"

"What are you even talking of? Please, you are too familiar." Her quick perusal of the room told her that many were giving them a considerable amount of attention. "Behave yourself, Mr. Wickham."

"You don't want me to behave, Miss Elizabeth. I'm not nearly as fun." His eyes gleamed, and she at once wished she'd never given him such leave to be so familiar. Someone was sure to overhear, and after Mr. Darcy, he seemed immediately less . . . authentic.

She finished the longest reel of all time while spending the whole of the set trying not to crane her neck after Mr. Darcy, who had not returned from his escape into the night.

Jane and Mr. Bingley were separated for a time. Jane danced with Mr. Lucas's son while Bingley danced with Charlotte Lucas. But their eyes were only for each other, and the more they were together, the more Elizabeth could see two truly happy people. It was inspiring and a bit condemning all at the same time.

With Mr. Wickham breathing inappropriate comments down her neck and Mr. Darcy captivating her in every way as a truly good and noble person, she realized that no man was offering her something as wholesome as what Jane and Mr. Bingley seemed to be creating. And she at once wished to escape into the night like Mr. Darcy had.

Not that she wished to see him, though she would not complain if she did. But she was ashamed of her wantonness.

They finished their set with a crowd of women giggling after a scrap of Mr. Wickham's attention. He kissed the back of her glove with promises in his eyes, promises she intended to thwart. She was done with the flirtations from such a man and decided that they were not at all harmless.

As soon as she could, she found Charlotte Lucas and dragged her into a corner. "What am I going to do?"

But her friend's face clouded, and she looked away.

"What is it?"

"I don't know what you want me to say, Elizabeth. You have two of the three handsome men in the room clamoring for your attention and you are coming to me with your girlish complaints. What should you do? You should secure your future and leave some scraps for the rest of us."

Elizabeth sucked in a breath and held it. Her friend was obviously unhappy about something specific. Or perhaps she was truly bothered by Elizabeth's good fortune. She waited, watching for Charlotte to elaborate. After a time, her friend sighed. "I apologize. I've received a letter from Mr. Collins."

"Ugly, annoying cousin Collins?" Elizabeth grimaced.

But Charlotte's face turned to stone. "You mustn't speak of him so."

A sense of dread filled Elizabeth's stomach.

"He's asked for my hand. Again."

"Even after you have once refused him?"

"Yes, he is most adamant that his feelings have grown stronger. He said Lady Catherine is most insistent that I am the perfect bride. And after tonight, when all men have eyes only for you or your sister, I am inclined to agree."

"You are not going to accept him!"

"I am. And in a fortnight, I will be travelling to Kent."

Elizabeth hugged her middle, watching her friend make a most disastrous decision certain to leave very little room for happiness in her life. "What can I say?"

"How about congratulations? I am to be married. Be happy for me."

Elizabeth nodded. "Of course." She hugged her friend close, tight, but Charlotte pulled away first, not really looking into her face.

"I wish you the best, most dear happiness you can possibly have." Elizabeth felt the words die on her lips. Mr. Collins was an abhorrent person. She herself had denied him.

"I have few prospects. It is time I became less of a burden on my dear parents. I will live out my days in security and with some measure of happiness. Which is more than you can claim at the moment."

The words felt sharp, and they reached places in Elizabeth's insecurities that she had forgotten nagged at her. But she could say nothing in return. Charlotte was correct. Elizabeth was not quite so desperate as to destroy her happiness in exchange for security. She had time yet to make rational choices.

A little bit of time.

Chapter Eight

Darcy woke the next morning with a pounding head and a restlessness that nothing could cure, so he took himself outside. The air was crisp. He didn't wait for his valet, flinging a shirt across his back, leaving the cravat at home. The jacket he slung over his shoulder would likely be left somewhere as the air heated. He needed to be out and walking.

As soon as he stepped out the door, he headed toward the highest hill. The area around Netherfield was mostly flat, but there was a sort of elevated hill that seemed close enough, so he walked in that direction. The hour was early. No one but the tenants would be out. He was left to his own woolgathering, which was intense indeed. He couldn't stand to be within the same walking distance of George Wickham. Ordinarily he would have left Netherfield last night, Bingley or no. But here he was, taking in the cool morning air, shared with George.

Curse Wickham. What was he doing in this town? What was he doing asking Miss Elizabeth to dance?

And was it his imagination or could there have been a sense of intimacy between them? Were they friends? Surely Wickham would not be pursuing her. Darcy knew the man too well to assume such a thing. From what Darcy could tell, Miss Elizabeth didn't offer anything to Wickham that he would find of use that would tempt him to tie himself down. So what was he doing sniffing around the Bennet family?

His hands fisted. Nothing good.

Perhaps Darcy should leave like he ought to have done last night?

But what of Miss Elizabeth? Even though nothing could come of a flirtation with her, he didn't wish her to be preyed upon by such a man. He, who knew what Wickham was capable of, he should step in to do something.

He told himself he was protecting her and her family and the entire village. But was he simply hoping to spend more time with the beguiling woman? Thoughts of her were distracting him at every turn. Her eyes would smile at him in his mind, or her laugh chide him no matter what he did or thought. Sleep stayed far away when there was a distraction such as her to keep him company.

He walked for an hour before reaching the base of the small elevation, and then laid his jacket in the brush to continue the climb. His feet picked up their pace. What he wanted was an intense round of boxing at Jackson's. Or a really good run. He stretched out his stride and picked up his pace until his heart was pounding and his feet were complaining from inside his boots, but he pushed until he reached the top. As he came around a bend, a soft body ran into his chest. His arms reached out, catching her, cradling her from a fall. Citrus and lavender rose up in the air around him. *Miss Elizabeth?*

Her head was down and her bonnet obscured most of his face. "My apologies, miss. Have I hurt you?"

Wonder and relief filled him when Miss Elizabeth's face turned up to meet his. He pulled her closer. "Oh, Miss Elizabeth, I'm terribly sorry. Are you well?" His hands rand up and down her back and he hugged her, not believing it was really her.

And she allowed it for a moment. Then she stepped away. "What are you doing up here, Mr. Darcy?" Her eyes traveled over his attire and focused in on his open neck line.

But he could do nothing about his state of undress. "I felt some good exercise was in order. And you?" He held out a hand, indicating that she, too, was at the top of the hill—from the looks of it, alone. He swallowed twice before he felt free to look at her, knowing they were well and truly alone.

"I needed a good walk as well. I've been pacing the floor

half the night. And this . . . this seemed like the only remedy."

"What ails you?" He reached out and tucked a bit of hair behind her ear. "I, too, have been up half the night."

She stepped nearer, and for a moment he thought she might open up. Her lips parted, her eyes filled with sincerity and hope. But then she pressed them together and turned away. "I could ask the same of you, then. Really, Mr. Darcy. You are half dressed." She let her eyes travel over his open chest, his bare neck, and back up to his face, leaving a trail of warmth he was uncertain how to squelch.

"You say those words with disdain, but your eyes speak otherwise." He reached for her hand. "As if . . . as if you might be enjoying my disarray?"

When his skin touched hers, she caught her breath and he smiled.

She snatched her hand away. "I'm uncertain what is so amusing to you here."

"Nothing." He dipped his head. "I'm not amused. But I *am* pleased. You make me happy, in every way. And I'm attempting not to be so caught by you, but I am finding you difficult to resist."

Her lips parted again. He stepped closer. He might not be able to prevent his mouth from covering those soft lips. They begged to be kissed properly. He forced himself to look away.

His jaw worked and his teeth ground together. After

several breaths, he turned back to her. "Please tell me what is so troubling that you are up here at the brink of daylight alone."

She moved to the ridge, looking out over all the land around them. "I'm uncertain, to be honest. What brings you here? I would really like to know."

He hesitated and then gave in. "You."

She went completely still.

He stood at her side. The view was magnificent. And she was the same. His heart pounded in his chest. His hands clenched and unclenched several times, and then he gave in to what he wanted most. "I am about to tell you something that I should probably keep to myself. I should lock the words inside and just leave this minute for Pemberley, but I find I cannot. My heart dictates their being spoken, now." He sounded quite emotional. He almost didn't recognize himself, but there was nothing for it. He physically could not keep the words inside.

She faced him, her expression almost too much for him in its open expectation.

"Please know I say the following only with your best interest at heart."

She nodded, her brow wrinkling a moment, then clearing.

"George Wickham is a man to be avoided at all costs."

Her mouth dropped open and then her eyes narrowed, and he at once knew he'd made some incredibly daft blunder, but he wasn't too certain what it could be. She stepped closer. "And why is that, Mr. Darcy?"

"I'm afraid I cannot divulge the source of my knowledge, but his character is not to be trusted; he is not to be trusted. I would not wish the worst vixen upon him."

"And what are you suggesting? That I avoid him altogether? Give him the cut direct?"

"Whatever it takes to convince him that you are not interested in his company."

"Just like that?"

"Like what? Yes. I think it would be very wise. Certainly, don't dance further with him. He was very familiar . . ." Darcy wished to take back those words. In speaking them, he admitted to watching their dance, even though he'd left the assembly hall. In truth, he'd circled back, watching in the window. He'd not been able to resist knowing just how familiar she was with the deplorable George Wickham.

Her face went white. "And you have come up here to tell me this?"

"No. I—I came up here to think. I am telling you because you are here and it seems the correct thing to do . . ." He ran a hand through his hair, something he hadn't done since his early days at Eton. "Was I incorrect in warning you?"

"What? Oh, I can't say, can I? I must take your word that a man we've all known for a time, much longer than we've known you, is not to be trusted. I'm to believe you simply because you speak the words? To hear the man who asked for a meaningless flirtation express to me his opinion on the merits of another man?" She clucked. "I find it difficult to take you seriously."

"Why would you not? Have I shown a lack of good judgment or a fault in character?"

She tipped her head. "One could argue such a thing."

He stiffened. How could she find fault in him? He'd done nothing but treat her with respect and interest. He'd been honest in his availability and communicated openly about wanting to know her better. "Perhaps you are enamored with him; he's beguiled you already and you are finding him hard to resist?" The words came out as poison on his lips.

She tipped her head back and laughed. "Oh, Mr. Darcy. You don't have any idea of what you speak. And you have no right, you who have known me so little, you who have expressed an interest yourself, to dictate anything to me. I'll dance with whom I like, when I like." She stepped away. "And now, if you'll excuse me, I'll continue the walk I meant to take alone." She walked away from him toward the back side of the hill.

"Wait. No, Miss Elizabeth. Allow me to explain. To apologize?" he called after her, and when he said the word "apologize," she paused.

"I'm a blunder head."

Her mouth twitched.

"No, I'm worse than that. I'm an overstepping ogre with a large amount of pride?" He watched her.

She half turned.

"Who just wants an excuse to keep you close, to keep you talking, so he can look into your beautiful eyes a moment more."

She fully faced him, but instead of loving, hopeful eyes, hers were full of skepticism. "I don't need your falsity, sir. I know I'm not the most beautiful woman in the world. I know I have little to offer. I also know that I am difficult at times. But you don't need to create niceties to share, thinking they will soften my opinions."

He dipped his head in acknowledgement. "It is a hard thing, indeed, to think I may have lost your good opinion."

"It can be re-won. No good opinion is lost forever." She studied him. "Unless yours would be?" Something important hinged on his answer to this question. He wasn't certain what it could be, but he sensed he should respond honestly and carefully.

"I have said in the past that my good opinion once lost is lost forever. But in the case of you . . ." He stepped nearer, hardly daring to in case she would turn and run. "I do not think you could lose my good opinion."

Her eyes widened, and she nodded slowly as he lifted her hand to his mouth.

This time his lips found her soft skin and pressed once, twice, three times in and around her knuckles. He wanted to turn her hand over and run fingers over the softness in her palms, but he waited.

"I will dance with Mr. Wickham if I so choose."

He started to shake his head, but then paused. He could never condone such a thing, but neither could he control it. "I don't recommend it. If I could tell you all that I know . . ." He paused.

Her eyes opened wide.

He knew she was waiting for him to reveal what he knew, to tell her something, anything, that would help her understand his odd request.

He ran a hand through his hair again in frustration. More people than he would suffer if the information were passed around. And so even if it might be the death of him, he must remain silent. Hopefully she would trust him enough. More than her life depended on it, really.

She bit her lower lip. Which of course was so distracting to Darcy that he almost forgot he was supposed to not think about kissing her. She seemed to ponder for too long a time before she lifted her long lashes. Her brilliant eyes shone back at him. "I think . . . we should talk of other things. Tell me of your home." She started walking slowly along the ridge, as though he would come walk beside her.

Which he could not do, could he? Could he simply ignore the fact that she was dismissing his warning? Why would he speak up if it were not important? How could she not take him seriously?

He stood in silence for many moments while she trailed fingers along low branches and meandered slowly about on the hilltop.

At last he turned. "Woman!"

She whipped around. "Mr. Darcy?"

He marched over to her. "I am unaccustomed to being dismissed so completely."

Her mouth twitched, but she said nothing.

"When I exert myself to assist someone, to share what I know . . ." He turned away, then turned back. "Most would listen more closely. I cannot impress upon your mind in strong enough language how important it is that you heed my warning."

The other side of her mouth twitched. And then she seemed to have mercy on him. "Oh, Mr. Darcy, I am not dismissing you. I just think you are not entitled to lord over me. You have no say in my life and no responsibility over me. You are kind to care." She placed a hand on his forearm. "And I appreciate your concern." She stepped closer again. The wind carried up an intoxicating scent of lemons.

"I would not see you hurt or otherwise damaged. You . . ."

She ran her fingers up his arm.

"You are at risk."

She nodded. "I have thought the same." She placed her hand at his chest, just below the wide-open bare neckline.

He covered her hand with his own, his heart surely

pounding into her fingertips, revealing his great awareness of her skin near his, of the warmth through his shirt wherever she touched.

He reached out to tug on a pin keeping her hair captive. As soon as it was released, the locks fell down around her shoulders. She was magnificent.

"You have already suspected Wickham of treachery."

She nodded, looking up into his face, her eyes, her lips, her face and hair beguiling him, like a siren in the sea, inviting him closer.

He was powerless to resist. If she wished it, he would have done all she asked.

Chapter Nine

How was it possible for one woman to feel so many different things at once? Elizabeth did not know how she could resist such a man. But she also could not abide his interference. And she was plagued with curiosity. What had Mr. Darcy discovered of Mr. Wickham that would motivate him to express such a low opinion of another? Surely he was not prone to gossip? As soon as she was back home, she would immediately employ Jane to help her discover his secrets.

Mr. Darcy lifted her hand so that the tips of her fingers brushed against his mouth. Then he pressed his lips to one tip. "Your hands. They are so soft." He kissed another. "Might I tell you my thoughts the first time I kissed your hand?"

She nodded, tingles running through her hands, distracting all other sensation, only allowing for partial thought. He traced the lines of her hand with one finger and then lifted the palm to his mouth, pressing his lips in the exact center.

He leaned closer to whisper, "I cursed your gloves."

She giggled, and then wished to bite back the noise, but admitted, "I did as well. Wished to pull them off and throw them into the flames."

"Did you?" He grinned, his lips turning up into a rather wicked but pleased grin.

Elizabeth wished to devour it in one crush of her mouth. "And why is such a thing good news to you?"

He kissed another finger. "No reason." His attention to her hands did not stop. One finger at a time, he kissed her, again and again until her knees threatened to sink beneath her, and Elizabeth reached a hand out to cling to his arm.

"You are too much."

He shook his head. "Not too much. Just the right amount, perhaps?" His eyes shone with mischief over the top of one of her knuckles, which he caressed with a soft slow circle and occasional kisses.

She could not let this man have such control. How was he any different from any other cad she might meet? She closed her eyes. "And what if Wickham were to do such a thing? What if he were here instead of you?"

He dropped her hand as though it were a hot coal, and stepped away.

A bit troubled but somewhat relieved to be able to think

again, she laughed nervously. "Can you see what I'm saying? Why is our proposed flirtation any different from what Wickham might want?"

His face turned to stone; his eyes went cold. He adjusted his shirt and stepped further away. "If you cannot see a difference between me and George Wickham, then I am wasting my time indeed."

Her heart pained her, right in the center of her chest. But it had to be said. "You and he offer the same privilege, sir." She dipped her head. "Perhaps I was wrong to agree to such a thing. Have I lost your respect for this? Because I may have lost some for myself."

He shook his head. "I think we must be finished here, do you agree?"

A slow coldness seeped into the air around her. She nodded. "I think we must."

Then she watched as the most handsome and eligible man of her acquaintance walked away, disgusted with her. Why had she compared him to Wickham? Why had she thrown that in his face?

Because he had been getting to her, because she was afraid. He didn't want more than a flirtation. And she was swiftly wanting to spend the rest of her life with him. And that was probably the most fearsome situation of all. So she pushed him away, sort of.

He turned the corner and left her alone on the hillside. Why was it so abhorrent to be George Wickham? Granted, she knew Darcy was nothing like that weasel of a man. The difference between them was so stark and obvious, she hoped never to associate with the Wickham variety of man again. But that difference was a feeling more than anything else. She couldn't quite point to why Mr. Darcy was so far above Mr. Wickham in every way. And in comparing them, something told her she'd just insulted Mr. Darcy in the worst possible manner.

A cold worry crept into her thoughts. Perhaps she'd hurt him; perhaps she'd done damage to a good man.

And what an excellent flirtation it might have been. He was everything she'd wanted in a man so far. And he challenged her. And he was intelligent. What she would give to talk to him about literature. She assumed him to be very well read. Her father had the library envied by all in their small town. But Mr. Darcy probably out read him in every way.

Her shoulders slumped. But he was not free to love another. He was not free to participate in more than a flirtation. He'd been open about things. The whole thing tasted a bit sour now that Wickham had become part of the conversation. Perhaps a tiny part of her heart hoped that Mr. Darcy was as enamored as she might become, that he would forget whatever his prior obligations were that held him and would declare his love and intentions to court her.

She sighed as she began her slow descent.

By the time she arrived back at Longbourn, she was well and truly depressed.

Her feet dragged into the front room. She lifted her bonnet and handed it to Hill. Her sisters were conversing in the kitchen, but there was some conversation in the sitting room that sounded low and friendly. She turned to Hill.

"Mr. Bingley, miss, and a Mr. Darcy."

She went red with embarrassment.

"Are you well, miss?" Hill placed her hand on Elizabeth's face. "Have you caught a fever?"

"I'm well. More or less. Thank you, Hill." She brushed her hands down her dress. How had he come to be visiting in her parlor? How had Bingley come to be there? She paused in the doorway, then stepped into the room.

Mr. Darcy stood. He was dressed in a crisp cravat, his jacket neatly pressed, his hair not a bit out of place and his expression formal. Her skirts were covered in sticks and leaves, her hair a disheveled mess and her cheeks flushed from exertion. Life was simply not fair to the fairer sex. She lowered herself in a curtsy. "Mr. Darcy, Mr. Bingley."

Mr. Bingley started and leapt to his feet. "It is so good to see you, Miss Elizabeth."

"Thank you." She nodded.

Jane smiled, and then the two of them continued conversing as though they were the only people in the world. And perhaps they were. In their world. But her world included their entire front room, with a very stiff and formal Mr. Darcy. She approached him. "I'm surprised to see you here."

He indicated that they might sit, so she joined him on the sofa, leaving plenty of room between them. But he closed the space immediately and sat right at her side. "I don't know why you would be surprised. I have been here in this area for one reason only. To support my friend." He looked over his shoulder at a very close Mr. Bingley and Jane.

"I see."

He cleared his throat. "I admit to being pleased to be here for a time for other reasons than my friendship with Bingley." He nudged her.

"I have been thinking about our conversation. You seem far more offended than the conversation merited. There is much more going on there than simply being compared to a cad. Though I am sorry I made that comparison."

"So you admit that he is one?"

"Of course he is. Anyone with any sense can see that."

His face turned sad. "Not anyone. Some people with sense are completely blinded by his charms."

"It sounds like there is a story there; perhaps it might help me understand?"

"There is a story. A sad, almost disastrous tale. But it is someone else's and I am not free to share it." He wiped a hand down his face. "It pains me to speak of another in such a manner. I had hoped that perhaps we shared a mite more trust. But I can see that with such a small acquaintance, trust would be difficult."

She sighed. The truth was she did trust him. She trusted him enough to engage in the most vulnerable and brave flirtation, with no hope of any feelings ever reciprocated. But she couldn't tell him that. She had to remain the tiniest bit in control of her emotions as she studied his handsome face. She knew that seeing him more would only increase the chances of her falling in love with him. "I don't think trust is the issue."

He didn't speak for a long time, and she didn't look at him. The silence was long and felt thick, but when she finally broke it, she spoke of pleasantries only. His eyes were full of compassion and kindness. He rested his arm on the back of the sofa behind her, not quite touching her, but it felt much like an embrace even so. And she spent one small moment indulging the thought of a life with such a strong man's shoulder always available. The thought almost brought pain in its unrealistic possibility. It could never be, and that was the worst thought. She feared something quite disastrous. She might never meet another man she respected quite as much.

Chapter Ten

That evening, Darcy and Bingley began a game of billiards at Bingley's new residence, Netherfield.

Bingley lifted his stick. "She is the loveliest woman of my acquaintance. You must agree with me, Darcy. She's an angel."

"I would never disagree."

"And her sister. Miss Elizabeth." His friend eyed him. "You left rather abruptly after your second set. But you seemed to converse openly in their home . . ."

Darcy hit the next ball harder than he meant. It jumped over one and then hit the opposite side of the table, not really making an impact at all.

Bingley raised an eyebrow. "So it did not go well?"

He grunted while Bingley made his shot, dunking two balls on the opposite side of the table.

"Come, man. What happened? You caused a stir at the

assembly, you know. You choose a woman immediately, dance the first two sets with Miss Elizabeth, and then walk out straight after. The lady has a reputation to maintain."

Darcy tapped his stick on the floor. "We danced the first two sets. That should be sufficient to secure her in good opinion, I would think."

Bingley didn't look convinced.

"But there is nothing to worry about in that regard. I'm certain Miss Elizabeth and I will not be seeing each other more than we have to."

"You will have to, of course. Miss Bennet and I need as much time as possible together, and the only way that is possible is if you cooperate and spend time at the Bennet house or, at the very least, with Miss Elizabeth."

Darcy took off his jacket and undid his cravat. His friend was correct, of course. But did he care overly much if Bingley and Miss Bennet were able to spend time together?

Bingley had been happier than he'd ever seen him since meeting Miss Bennet. He skipped and whistled and sang and was completely enamored with the woman as far as Darcy could tell, but was she worthy of his friend's high esteem? What kind of family were the Bennets? He didn't know and perhaps should not interfere in such things. He was only looking for a way to avoid Miss Elizabeth. How could the woman assume any similarities at all between him and Wickham? At least she admitted the man was a cad. What she didn't know was that he was almost responsible for the complete ruin and unhappiness of Darcy's much beloved sister.

"What exactly are your designs on Miss Bennet?" Darcy watched Bingley.

"I don't have designs on her. Come, man. That sounds so conniving. I am merely interested in the woman—hope to know her better, court her, and marry her." He grinned, and Darcy knew that even though he sounded lighthearted, he was in fact completely serious. He would be pursuing Miss Bennet.

"I wish you all the happiness in the world."

"You approve, then?"

"Do you need my approval?"

"No. I don't." He stood taller. "But I'd like it all the same."

"Then very well. I approve. She is a lovely woman and you two seem suited. The next step would, of course, be to know the family."

"Then we must call on them every day this week."

Darcy took two breaths before responding. "I think that perhaps you should pay a visit every day this week. I might join you on your walks and at dinners and things, but I see no need for me to also come to know the family or for them to know me."

"That is sensible, of course. You must not be seen as courting the sister."

"Correct."

Bingley was quiet for a long time.

Darcy at last raised a hand. "Speak, man. What is it you want to say?"

"I wonder if perhaps you take your responsibilities to your aunt too seriously. Are you certain your mother wished for you to marry Anne? Are you certain that you cannot simply be free to pursue whom you wish?"

"No, I am not certain. But even if I were free, is Miss Elizabeth the woman I would pursue?"

"Is she?"

Darcy was about to say no, but then he thought about her wit, her beauty, her humor, and her smile, and he couldn't bring himself to deny the attraction. But attraction was one thing, inviting her to be the mistress of his estate another. He thought of sitting near her in her front room. The softness of her shoulder, the lovely turn of her neck. He admitted to himself only that he'd love to spend many an evening in her company sitting thus. There were several good books on the nearby table he would love to peruse.

"Let's stop by tomorrow, shall we?" he said.

"Excellent."

"We can offer to go for a walk."

The next day, they rode their horses to the Bennet home. A servant took them as soon as they dismounted and approached the front door. They were led into the front room, where five women stood.

He and Bingley bowed smartly, and the women all curtsied. The Bennet sisters looked somewhat alike. But the eldest were the most attractive.

Miss Bennet smiled. "We are so happy you could come. I'm sorry my father and mother are out, but you are welcome to join us here in the sitting room."

Bingley immediately moved to sit at Jane's side.

Darcy, however, suddenly felt closed in. He hesitated before he sat.

Miss Elizabeth approached. "Perhaps you'd care for a turn about our gardens?"

He nodded, grateful. "Yes. I'd like that."

She led the way out the front door and to the right. Then he stepped closer, walking at her side. "The weather is so inviting, it seems a crime to waste it indoors," he said.

"I agree. I walk every day if I can, even in a light rain."

He nodded. "You can find me out of doors most often as well. Our walk the other day was a good one. Good exercise up the last high bit and views all around." He cleared his throat. "I quite enjoyed the company."

She glanced at him. "Although, the company was not as lovely as it could have been."

"Perhaps we can begin again? Forget talk of Wickham?"

"I think I'd like that, at least to spend more time with you."

He stepped closer and offered his arm, which she took immediately.

"I do apologize for comparing you to such a man."

"Let's not speak of it again."

She held his arm with both of hers. "Agreed." She seemed tense, as if she wished to speak, then her next words blurted out. "But you do know you are a far better man than he is. You are the sun, where he is a candle flickering . . ."

Her skin was soft, her body melted into him at his side. Her steps matched his. He could spend many an afternoon exactly thus. "I think we shall be together often."

"I think you are correct." She smiled. "The thought is pleasant to me. I hope the same for you."

"Yes, I was just thinking that I shall not complain of such a thing. Bingley is most intent upon convincing your sister of his worthiness."

"And she is most happy to accept his convincing." Miss Elizabeth laughed. "They are the most perfect pair. Do you think either of them will ever be displeased with the other?"

"No, I do not." He placed a hand over hers. "Unlike us, who have already managed such a thing."

She sighed. "I often think that Jane will be the most happy of all of us, as she is the most deserving of happiness."

"I cannot agree she is the most deserving."

"Do you feel you are more?"

"No, as a matter of fact, I was thinking of you. If I could, I would work to ensure *your* happiness."

She was quiet for a long time. "You should not say such things."

"Why not, if they are true?"

She stopped. "What are we, Mr. Darcy?"

She gazed up at him, her lip caught between her teeth, one hand still on his arm, the other looking as though she didn't know quite how to place it.

He stepped nearer. What were they? "I remember us talking about a flirtation? About friendship? An understanding that I am unable to commit to anything is important."

"But is that what you want? Not to commit?"

They were close now, nearer than before. And he didn't know how to respond. Dare he be honest?

Her eyes flashed, daring him.

"What do I want?" He reached out and ran a finger along her forehead, tucking a hair behind her ear, admiring her face, her features, her mouth. "I would like to get to know you and keep getting to know you for a long, long time." He cupped the side of her face, his thumb caressing her cheek, growing closer to her mouth.

Miss Elizabeth closed her eyes and parted her lips, just a small amount, just enough that they looked full and tempting. He should have looked away, but he did not. His thumb crept closer to her lips, and then over to the soft pink of her mouth. He ran it gently, softly, across her lower lip.

Her eyes flashed open. She rested her hand on his chest, stepping nearer still. "But we don't always get what we want?"

He nodded, sure his pain showed in his eyes. “No, we don’t. And so, this is all I can offer.” He leaned closer, his lips close to her cheek, almost there. “If you will allow.”

She went very still. And then she nodded.

His lips brushed her cheek, a feather of a touch, but she leaned into him, her fingers climbing higher along his chest.

He wrapped his arms around her, pulling her close, pressed up against him. He buried his nose in her neck, breathing in lemons and lavender and feeling the delicate softness of her skin. Then he lifted her chin, just enough that he could stare into her face, so that her lips were near, the puff of her breath temptingly close.

Her eyes were welcoming, soft, caring. She lifted a hand to his face. But the expression was tender, hopeful. This woman didn’t want him for his kisses. She was losing her heart to him. Her trust undid his designs. She stood on her toes, stood as close as possible, parted her lips. The slightest shift, and his mouth could capture hers. She waited. He paused, the greatest agony of his life pounding through his heart with each beat.

His head shaking, his heart rebelling against the trueness of his thoughts, he murmured all sorts of things, but the only audible words said were, “I’m sorry.”

She clutched the fabric at her breast, stepped back two steps, and caught her breath. “I don’t understand.”

“I cannot do it. I cannot entertain a kiss from such a

worthy lady. My heart will be lost forever, and yours . . . I would never forgive myself for what I might do to yours."

She swallowed visibly. Her eyes flashed and she stood taller. "There is no worry about doing damage to mine, sir." She ran a hand swiftly down her skirts as though to wash him from her person. She turned. "I think I shall return to the house."

He made a move to offer his arm, but she shook her head and held up her hand. "That won't be necessary."

Darcy was left watching her retreating form with a torrent of emotions racing and circling through him.

Chapter Eleven

Elizabeth and Mr. Darcy had made their way quite a distance from home. She stomped her way through the brush, trying to rid herself of every frustration. But even decided and firm, walking did nothing to relieve her emotions. Every possible feeling raged through her in a torrent of swirling confusion. She tore a leaf from a branch, tossing it to the ground when she thought of his pride, his high and mighty sense that he got to decide if their flirtation should end.

She cringed and stopped walking altogether when she thought of her wanton closeness, her near begging for that kiss. What must he think of her? And then to have such an obvious advance refused. "Agggh." She wrenched a branch off a bush and tossed it aside. To think that she'd almost lost herself to such a man. That she was half in love with him already. And he did not feel the same. He had no such strong feelings for her. He was not ready to toss the flirtation aside and be real. Turned out, he was not even ready to have the flirtation at all.

Her cheeks flamed. She had thought that perhaps he wanted more.

But his admission that he was not ready to ignore whatever kept him from her because of the strength of his love hurt her. It was an irrational hurt, but how often was hurt rational? She told herself that his limitations were likely serious, that he was well and truly unavailable. But her irrational brain, which was currently in full control of her reckless half run down the hill, told her that if she were worthy enough in his eyes, he would lose everything for her, that he would deny whatever claims on his future and give himself to her. Or at the very least, kiss her when such a gift was offered.

But what did he even know of her? What did she know of him? She sighed. Her feet slowed. And some tiny inkling of the rational mind returned. Would she ever know him now that she'd stomped away in a huff?

Her shoulders slumped, and she trudged the rest of the way home. She would not. And perhaps that was for the best. She was far more suited for flirtations with the likes of George Wickham, a man who could mean nothing more to her ever, than with a man such as Mr. Darcy, from whom she might never recover her heart.

She pushed through the side door and into her house,

looking for a servant. No one seemed to be about. Her sisters were not heard or seen. Jane and Mr. Bingley had obviously not returned from what she assumed was their own walk. Where was everyone? She needed to divest herself of all her outer layers. The room felt overly warm.

A servant entered the front room, where she was depositing her bonnet and shawl. "A Mr. Wickham to see you, miss." He bowed and left, George Wickham standing in his place, a wicked and devilish grin on his face. "You're looking well."

Elizabeth laughed. "Oh, say what you will; I know I look a sight."

He stepped closer. "No, I am in earnest. Your cheeks are flushed, your hair giving hints of the wilder side to Miss Elizabeth." He reached out to untuck a bit of hair from behind her ear. "I would give a lot to see all these lovely locks unpinned." His eyes flashed with a certain hunger she'd seen in him before and for the most part brushed aside. It stirred something deep inside her, something foreign and a bit delicious.

But also uncomfortable.

She compared him to Darcy. She couldn't help it. Wickham was left entirely wanting. While Darcy also stirred something delicious, he had rejected an offer for a kiss. Her stomach clenched in embarrassment. Why reject her? Mr. Wickham was perfectly happy to flirt with abandon. Elizabeth had asked nothing of Darcy. She stood taller, fueled by her embarrassed resentment. And then she reached back into her thick hair and pulled out a single pin.

Mr. Wickham's eyes flamed. His eyes caressed her.

A thick section of her hair fell down past her shoulders, reaching her waist.

"You would be irresistible if men could see you just like this." He lifted a hand to her face and ran a finger along her forehead.

She raised her eyebrows, a sudden wicked urge fueling her. "Am I not already?"

He took his time, letting his mock inspection linger for long moments along her neckline, at her ear, down her arms. "Why do you think I'm here? The regiment is swimming in the water hole this afternoon. Please do not share that news with your sisters. And yet, here I stand, alone, at your bidding." His breath came faster. He reached out, lifted the freed section of hair, and brought the ends to his lips. "You are most captivating."

She reached for another pin.

Wickham stepped closer. He lifted his hand. "May I?"

Elizabeth swallowed and then nodded.

He pulled at a pin in just the right way, so that the sensations up and down her head were deliciously tingly. Another section of her hair fell down past her shoulders.

"Beautiful. As I knew it would be. Will you be chastised by your maid if I free every lock of your hair?" He tugged at another pin, allowing more to fall past her shoulders.

She didn't know how to respond, precisely. Here was Wickham, saying and doing the very things Darcy should have said and done. Her anger fueled her desire to let the moment play out, come what may. But the difference between the two men was apparent, and as she thought of the light in Darcy's eyes, his infuriating goodness, even his rejection, the tension of the moment squelched. She shook her head, opening her mouth to say something, anything, to get this man to stop his confusing attentions.

And then their servant announced, "A Mr. Darcy to see you, miss."

Elizabeth sucked in a breath too loudly, sounding mostly like a strangled gasp, a guilty gasp. Wickham stood frozen still. Darcy, too, had stopped his entrance, staring at the two of them. His eyes took in her hair, a flash of hurt tearing through Elizabeth's heart, then his eyes turned to stone as he looked at Wickham.

Wickham lifted three fingers. "Fitzwilliam." His insolent tone and the use of Mr. Darcy's first name were astonishing to Elizabeth, so much so that she forgot herself and asked, "You would be so familiar?"

Both men ignored her. And then Darcy said nothing more, did not spare her a second glance, and turned from the room.

Elizabeth heard the door open and close. "No!" She ran after him, bits of her hair trailing behind her. She flung the door open, the sound of it banging against the wall behind causing Mr. Darcy to stop, but he didn't turn, and then he picked up his pace.

But Elizabeth was not going to allow him to simply stomp away out of her life while thinking ill of her. "Wait."

But he continued to walk.

Luckily for Elizabeth, his horse was tied in the stables and not available to leap on and ride away. "Wait, please."

Wickham exited the front door, chasing after her until he reached for her arm. "What's this? Are you running after him, Elizabeth?"

She paused, but did not turn to look at him.

"You know you will never get anything out of that man. He is completely tied by purse strings and great-aunt strings."

She jerked away. "Just what do you think I hope to get out of that man? I simply wish for him to not think ill of me."

"And why would he? For speaking with me?"

"We were not merely speaking in his eyes, I'm sure."

Mr. Darcy was about to turn the corner and out of sight.

She dislodged her arm from Mr. Wickham. "Please. Allow me."

He dipped his head, a small insolent smile tugging at his lips. But he stepped away, saying nothing more.

A servant came running with Mr. Darcy's horse. She

leapt up on it, riding astride the saddle in her many skirts, and then she tore after him on his glorious stallion.

It took a matter of moments and she was upon him. “Mr. Darcy,” she breathed out, her heart pounding. “Please, we must talk.”

“No, Miss Bennet, we are not required to do anything, least of all talk. But I will thank you for bringing me my horse. If you please . . .” He stepped forward with a hand on his horse’s flank. “Do you require assistance dismounting?” He kept his eyes firmly away from her legs, which were almost bare, many of her skirts stretching too far across, the area at her ankles plainly visible.

Chapter Twelve

Darcy was not certain what to do with this woman. On the one hand, he'd like to leap up on the horse behind her, wrap his arms around her, and ride away somewhere private. That almost kiss was still doing things to him, things that only a long cold swim in the pond would cure. And she sat with eyes blazing, masterfully controlling his usually temperamental horse. She was a fine woman indeed. If he were but free to pursue any woman of his choice . . . Thoughts like that one were not productive in the slightest. Instead he should be considering how to assist his aunt, how to help her daughter in ways that didn't involve anything romantic. One entrapment was enough for a person's life.

He tugged on his jacket, straightening it as if to straighten his thoughts. "What are you doing?"

"I'm riding your horse."

He fought the sudden urge to smile. "I see that. And why are you riding him?"

"Because you were ignoring me." She huffed. "And we need to talk." She tried to lift up and over the saddle horn, but paused when her skirt tore the slightest bit. She turned a lovely shade of pink before replacing her leg. "I'm in a bit of a quandary."

"Would you like some assistance?"

"I don't know what you can do. I shall just have to stay up here until I return to our barn. And you, sir, can stay right there so we can talk."

Her sweet embarrassment, her energy, the very air she breathed seemed more refreshing than any of the life Darcy lived. Could he have a conversation with this woman and remain on the sane side of normal? Could he resist anything truly damaging to her reputation?

Well, anything damaging beyond riding on the same horse? He laughed to himself, and then recklessly leapt up behind her. "No one will see, come." He reached around her shocked-into-silence body and grabbed the reins. "Hiyah, Samson!"

His horse responded immediately and took off at a full gallop along the path through the trees.

Her body relaxed against him. Which should not have surprised him, but he was even more pleased with her. He nuzzled through her luxurious hair, murmuring, "Where can we go where we won't be noticed?"

She rested her hands over his on the reins, and then he allowed her to guide them both. She was an expert horsewoman. Her legs squeezed up against Samson and the horse responded. She leaned one way with a gentle tug on the reins, and it was as if the horse read her mind. Darcy could not be sure, but at one point it seemed as though she told the horse nothing at all and he still turned. They approached a rather steep hill. Darcy thought they would pause at the bottom by a stream, but she leaned forward and said something to Samson, who leapt forward and raced up the hill, completely in control of the reins.

Miss Elizabeth laughed into the wind and he shook his head. "You are too good for bedlam. But I have to wonder . . ."

She held her arms out and tilted her head back, and it was all he could do not to circle her waist with his hands and pull her back up against him.

"Try it! Let go of whatever it is that holds you so tightly wrapped," she shouted back to him. His horse kept up the galloping madness, and Elizabeth's arms stretched in her declaration of freedom. So he did what only a man enthralled with such a woman would do. He held his hands out and shouted into the wind.

It blew by him, his body feeling more attuned to the rhythm of his horse than ever before. With his only connection to the horse his thighs, he allowed himself to roll and rock with the smooth flying gallops of the brilliant animal.

Elizabeth leaned back into him, and the two of them, arms out into the breeze, rode the beautiful stallion all the way to the top of the hill.

When Samson crested the top, he lifted his front legs into the air with a triumphant whinny. Elizabeth called out and grabbed the horn. Darcy threw his arms tighter around her and gripped the reins. But instead of shrinking in fear, she laughed and leaned forward to pat Samson. "That's a good boy."

Her hair fell down around her shoulders in shimmery waves. Her eyes were bright, her lips full. He was more than captivated by this beautiful woman, and he didn't know what to do about the sudden strong urge to capture those lips with his own. They were full and inviting and smiling up at him as if in invitation. His arms still encircled her. She was almost close enough as she turned to face him.

"Miss Elizabeth." His voice was soft, gentle to his own ears.

"Mr. Darcy." Hers was teasing, lilting, smiling with energy while she spoke.

He knew what she was going to do before she urged Samson forward again, this time at a walk. "Come on, boy. Show us something beautiful up here."

His horse snorted and snuffled and kicked his feet a little as if answering her, and then moved forward at a slow ambling walk.

"I do believe you've charmed my horse. The living, walking traitor of a beast."

"All you have to do is give him a little adventure. He'll eat out of your hand." She reached forward to pat him again. "Isn't that right, you beautiful animal? Don't listen to Mr. Darcy. He's just going to hand you off to his stable hand anyway."

"I do no such thing." He strained against his suddenly tight cravat. "At least not usually. I tend to his brushing down myself." He resisted adding, "Don't I, you good boy?" She was having an infernal effect on him, a strong one. But he didn't resist, not much.

She reached up and tugged on something in her hair and then brought out another pin. She smiled apologetically. "I guess I forgot that one."

And then the image of George Wickham with his hands in her hair came rushing back to him. He stiffened. "Or do you mean Mr. Wickham forgot that one?" He studied her face, watching for any sign of her feelings.

She blushed furiously, but her eyes were defiant. "You have no right to jest about such a thing."

"Don't I?"

"You absolutely do not. You who would not even accept an offer from me, you who would never dream of taking out a woman's pins, even when gifted the opportunity . . ."

He reached forward and ran his hand up the back of her head, his fingers running along her scalp with a hunger he knew was only growing. "I dream of it. It's never far from my thoughts, especially when you are right here."

She swallowed, and then ran her tongue along her lower lip.

"Confound it, woman. Stop."

Her lips dropped open.

His hand lowered to the back of her neck and he tugged her closer, just enough, to see if she would respond.

And she did. She leaned. Just enough. She didn't close the gap between them. She didn't place herself in kissing distance, but she did lean.

He searched her face. Oh, he wanted this woman. He wanted to kiss her madly. But he wanted her for more than that. And it was that want that stayed his urges. What would he do after he kissed her? How would he resist? How could he leave her, hoping for more when he knew he could not?

"Oh, stop your woolgathering. I'm not going to come asking for a proposal." She leaned closer, her eyebrow lifted in supreme delicious adventure.

He had to laugh in a low, earthy chuckle before tilting his head and at last covering her mouth with his own.

Samson shifted beneath them, but Darcy hardly noticed. His senses exploded in a great swarm of pure bliss. He didn't know what else to call it. Every part of him wanted to smile at once, but he concentrated on her mouth, took a little nibble on her lower lip. Her fingers dug into his arms. Then he kept pressing and pulling and kissing her with the kind of abandon he'd rarely felt in his life.

Her body leaned closer. She rested against him, one hand rising up along his chest to his shoulder and then into his hair. She fisted a handful at the back of his neck, which made him groan. One kiss would never be enough with this woman. One lifetime would not.

He pulled her closer, his mouth moving along hers in an intense desire to memorize its texture, to know her intimately, to be able to remember the feel of the velvety softness. Again and again his kissed her, until her mouth turned softer, lazier, her lips grew heavy feeling, her hands pulled at him in a helplessness he didn't know how to ease. This was it. This kiss would stop here on his horse and could progress no further. Their lives together could not be. But as he kissed her softness again and again, slowing down ever so gradually, he knew he would kiss her again. How could he not? How could he not devour her lips at every opportunity?

But she sighed in between his kisses and he paused. Then he rested his forehead against hers. "I don't think I'll ever be the same, Miss Elizabeth."

"Nor I." She tore off a glove and rested her fingers on her lower lip. "Nor my mouth." She laughed. "Does it look swollen to you?"

He studied her and again appreciated her wildly intense

beauty. "I've never seen a more beautiful woman." He cupped the side of her face.

Her gaze met his with such a warm and caring glow that he was stunned at the holiness of the moment. How could one feel closer to light and goodness while kissing a woman?

"But are they swollen?" She smiled.

"You look deliciously mussed. Your hair, your lips, all of it looks as though you have been kissed properly." He pressed his lips into her hair. "And you smell of cinnamon."

"Do I?" She leaned up against him. "I suppose that is good, then."

"In my opinion, it is the very best to be kissed properly and smell of cinnamon." He encircled her in his arms, her back up against his chest, and nudged Samson to keep walking. They followed the paths along the top of the hill, the wind circling in the air around them, not strong enough to chill or entangle her hair, but cool enough to keep the heat away. She snuggled into him and sighed. "Could there be a more perfect day?"

"If it did not have to end . . ."

She held up a hand. "Don't ruin it, not yet."

He rested his chin on the top of her head, holding his peace. But his heart had already begun to ache at the thought of leaving her side.

Chapter Thirteen

Elizabeth knew she was reckless. She knew she could not continue thus, kissing a man who was not her betrothed, riding alone with a man on the same horse, no less. But she also did not know how to resist this man. After such a kiss from such a man, how could she ever resist another kiss from Mr. Darcy? Did a kiss change a person? His certainly had. Or at least she felt changed.

She snuggled back into him, feeling his arms tighten around her. Was she wanton? A complete and utter disgrace? She did not care at the moment. She could not regret a single moment. She knew she would do it all again. And what if her heart was lost?

She tried to make an accounting of her potential for heartbreak. Her heart was certainly not in her possession at the moment. But tonight, when the magic of Mr. Darcy was far from her, she felt fairly certain her heart would once again be intact and in its proper location, beating with perhaps some longing, but that could be overcome. Surely.

As his arms cradled her and the smell of his soap filled the air around her, a delicious mix of sandalwood and spices, she planned to make it so. She willed her heart to be immune to his charm. Regardless, whatever happened tonight in the quiet of her room, it was worth this moment in his arms. Or so she told herself.

Samson meandered along as though understanding the need to take his time. She would have to thank this horse. Truly, he had become her new best friend in the animal world. Perhaps she could send a servant over with an extra portion of oats and alfalfa for him.

Mr. Darcy shifted behind her, and she could tell by the new tension in his chest that he was about to alter the mood of their ride. He cleared his throat. And then he was silent.

So she twisted to face him. They were close, their faces almost in kissing distance again, but she did not retreat. Instead, she tilted her head to the side. "Was there something you wanted to say?"

His face clouded, and then he smiled. "I haven't decided."

"You may as well just spit it out. I'll wonder."

He nodded and looked away, and then he ran a hand

through his hair. He appeared for a moment so endearingly vulnerable that she almost held his face in her hands and kissed him again. But instead, she waited.

When his eyes met hers again, he shrugged. "Wickham."

She nodded slowly. Of course he'd want to discuss Wickham. It was her turn to shift and feel uncomfortable. But her delay only increased the angst in his expression. Before he could close off entirely, she placed a hand on his arm. "Wickham means nothing to me."

He eyed her, apparently waiting for more of an explanation.

"I suppose it looked . . . odd to see us together, pins out of my hair."

He watched her, still waiting.

"Perhaps we have had a flirtation, in the past. Perhaps he has been seeking a continuation, an increase in our interactions. But he has never been bold enough to take out my pins. That was a new and, as I look back, unwanted attention."

Mr. Darcy stiffened.

And something about his reaction set Elizabeth's ire on fire. He had no right to have any feeling whatsoever about George Wickham. Or so she thought. But she tried to maintain an easy air about her words. "I do not go about kissing men. If that's what you're wondering."

He seemed partly mollified. But his reaction was not

sitting well with Elizabeth, not at all. "And you? Might I ask about others with whom you have engaged in a flirtation? Should I ask about your commitments elsewhere that keep you so entrapped?" She sat higher on Samson, up for this challenge.

But he closed off completely; his expression went blank, and gone was the easy, readable vulnerability in his face. "No, you may not. You are correct. This conversation is nobody's business." He reached for the reins and clucked to Samson, who picked up his pace. "And now, it is high time to return you to your family, hopefully with no one the wiser."

She sighed. "Very well." No matter what she did, she could not feel the same ease she'd had moments before. The intimacy they'd shared was missing. She leaned back into him, but while he didn't shift away, there was a certain stiffness that made the whole thing feel less cozy, less inviting. And eventually she sat up more and allowed a certain distance between them.

When they rounded the next bend, Darcy squeezed his thighs into Samson. "Hold on," he murmured into her ear, sending a new wave of pleasant gooseflesh over her skin and down her core. Samson responded immediately and took off at a graceful gallop across the remaining meadow at the top of the hill. The sun warmed them, the sky a brilliant bright blue. Elizabeth again laughed into the air.

Mr. Darcy turned them down the path and raced across the very meadow where they'd been. They took logs and creeks in leaps as Samson showed off his jumping ability until they were almost at her house. He at last came to a stop in the back behind the servants' barn. "I think you can proceed from here with safety and discretion?"

She nodded.

He slipped down and then lifted his hands up to assist her. She lifted one leg up and over and then adjusted her skirts with no embarrassment. His large palms gripped her waist and lowered her slowly to the ground. She looked up into his face. His eyes were tender. She smiled.

And then his mouth covered hers. He explored her lips like he'd never again taste them. She responded in kind, drinking in the sense of him, his smell, the feel of his hands, his mouth, the closeness they shared with Samson at her back. She wanted to remember this moment forever.

When he stopped, his lips still close enough to nibble if she chose, she nodded. "Thank you."

He rested his forehead against hers. "I will never be the same."

She could only close her eyes in acknowledgement of a similar feeling.

But then he stepped back and bowed. "Miss Elizabeth."

She curtsied, the new formality telling her more than words that this was their relationship and nothing more, nothing intimate or personal. A new burning lined her eyes, but she blinked it away as he climbed back onto Samson and, without another glance, rode away in the direction they'd come.

"Goodbye, then." She lifted her hand, her words heard by no one but herself.

When she stepped back into the house, coming in through the servants' kitchen entrance, the conversation paused. And the discomfort of servants specifically not saying things and obviously thinking something was a bit overwhelming. She nodded, trying not to feel guilty for her outing and telling herself she didn't answer to them anyway.

But as soon as she entered the more public part of the house, loud laughter carried over to her from the front sitting room. Even though she knew she looked a sight, her hair still hanging down past her shoulders, likely in knots, she turned to see what was so entertaining.

And then Lydia's shriek and Mary's disapproving grunt and Wickham's charming murmur picked up her pace as she burst into the room. But there was nothing untoward. A game of whist in the corner with Mary, Lydia, Kitty, and Mr. Wickham seemed to be the most innocuous part of the afternoon.

But Mr. Wickham raised his eyebrows in silence as his gaze perused her from head to toe. "You are looking well." His eyes danced with mischief and untold questions.

She could do nothing about the immediate blush that she felt take over her face and neck, which caused such a ridiculous laugh from their guest that she could only huff and turn from the room.

Their laughter at her expense carried out into the hall after her, but she ignored it, calling for a servant and a bath.

Chapter Fourteen

Mr. Darcy crumpled up a letter from his aunt. He wanted nothing more than to toss it into the fire, but he knew he must respond. He must do his duty. He must somehow erase the guilt of kissing Miss Bennet, of wanting to kiss her again. She did not deserve such treatment, kisses without promises, and yet, she'd wanted it as much as he.

But his cousin did not deserve such from him either—his unwell, sickly cousin who wrote him every week of her anticipation of their wedding, of the day he would come and rescue her from the bonds of such a mother, save her from the daily deluge of negativity in that house and move her to Pemberley with him, as his wife.

He cringed at the thought.

A rescue sounded like just the thing. Loving his cousin as a family member felt, too, like an appropriate thought.

But he could not get to the marrying part no matter how hard he tried, no matter what he did. He could not make himself happy about such an idea.

But how else he could rescue Lady Anne De Bourgh, he did not know.

And his aunt certainly had drilled into him his duty. His own mother had done the same before her death. Her dying words, in fact, would never leave Darcy's mind. "Please care for Anne. She does not deserve her treatment there. You are her only hope."

He had agreed, like any son would. "I will, Mother." His answer haunted him still.

And now he lived with the consequences. If he could only drum up the courage to at last do his duty, he could end the dread and simply live with the consequences.

But Miss Elizabeth's defiant eyes, their brilliant light, interrupted his resolve. Could he not love another woman? Marry her out of passion and love instead of resolve and duty? He feared not, as his father had already spent most of his living years drumming into Darcy the idea that he was not the master of his life, nor his soul, even. "You belong to Pemberley and it to you. We owe it to the people whose portraits line this hall." He'd pointed to a long line of venerable Fitzwilliams and Darcys. "And to our tenants. You must be master before you are mister." His life was never meant to be about what he desired.

As a young boy, Darcy had stood taller, sensing the

importance of such a birthright. But now that portrait hall seemed like a prison and nothing more, a line of disapproving expressions from a line of wardens intent on demanding from him, and not giving. He'd started taking the long way to his study to avoid such a walk down a hall that grew in length as the years progressed.

He reopened the crumpled letter from his aunt and then pulled out a new parchment. The quill, he dipped in ink filled with his lifeblood, or so it seemed. He scratched out the words, *My dear aunt, Lady Catherine. I will come at my earliest convenience.*

After penning a letter of promises he knew would pain him to keep, he announced to his servants his intent to leave in one day's time. And then Bingley bounced into his office. The man simply glowed with happiness. "She is the most glorious creature of my acquaintance."

Darcy smiled, though it pained him. He was happy for his friend, naturally, but that happiness came with the knowledge that he himself would never know such a feeling. "How are you in pursuit of the most angelic creature to walk this earth? Or so you've told me a dozen times."

"Things are perfectly perfect, if you must know. Her mother, her father, her sisters, all in support, or so it appears. And Jane, though I've not dared call her such, looks on me with such tenderness . . ." He seemed as though he might faint straight away from his own raptures.

"Have you declared yourself? Does she know how you feel?"

He tossed his hat on the couch and fell to its surface before running a hand though his hair in obvious frustration. "I have not."

"What is stopping you?"

"It is the woman herself." He laughed. "I stare into her face and I just know I don't deserve such an angel. Darcy, she doesn't even think ill of others. She defends them with every turn. I . . . I cannot think what marriage to me will be like to her."

At this, Darcy laughed out loud. "Do you not see yourself in your description? When have you ever criticized another? When do you yourself think ill? Bingley, come, man. If Miss Bennet were to have a twin, you would be it in congeniality and goodness."

His eyes lifted with such hope that Darcy could only shake his head. "Though I suppose it is healthy for you to have a decent amount of respect for the lady, you should feel free to pursue her. You offer her all that is good, as angelic as you claim she is."

"She is, trust my account of her goodness."

Darcy held up a hand. "I do. She is the angel you declare she is. You deserve such a woman. Trust your best friend in this."

He grabbed his hat. "I shall return to her home and tell her directly."

"Do."

He stopped. "No, I shan't yet. I shall tell her tonight."

"What is this evening?"

"A dinner party. You are to come. It is rather large. There shall be dancing."

Darcy had already begun shaking his head. "I'm off to Lady Catherine. She has demanded my presence." He held up the crumpled paper.

"Oh come, Darcy, surely you can attend one more party here before you go. Leave in the morning?"

He was not inclined to lengthen out his own misery, but the look on Bingley's face gave him pause. His friend needed him. He might do all manner of rash things, but still, he would have left, his aunt's petition holding sway over most things, until the thought of Miss Elizabeth teasing him, laughing even from across the room, was enough to give him pause. "I shall attend, but know, friend, the servants have been instructed that I leave at first light."

"I'll miss you, old friend."

"And I you. Come at your earliest convenience to Pemberley. You are always welcome, you know."

"Thank you. Might I . . . that is to say, should I . . . before you go, I'd like to know what you think of Miss Bennet?"

Darcy looked with envy on his happy friend, who could do nothing but repeat the same conversations with the same adulation of his love. “I think she is just as you describe, the most lovely creature in the world for you.”

His friend’s face looked as though it might burst with joy, so Darcy held up his hand. “But please, do not do anything overly bold. Get to know her, the family, the area. You have all the time in the world to explore this direction.” Darcy wished with all his soul to have the same luxury. “Declare yourself. Enjoy it, man.” He nearly choked on the last words, and looked down at his desk.

Bingley appeared as though he might say more, but Darcy pretended to be about the business of writing, though he’d said all he wished to say to his aunt.

Soon, Bingley left the room and Darcy replaced his pen, his gaze drifting to the lawn outside, his thoughts about two miles to the east in the home of Miss Elizabeth Bennet.

Chapter Fifteen

Hours later, the Bennet household was in a turmoil. Nothing too serious ever happened in Elizabeth's home, but you wouldn't know it by the wails and screeches that sounded down the hall. Something was amiss with Lydia's bonnet and she blamed Kitty, and Jane wouldn't share hers, and rightly so, for she'd given Lydia enough bonnets.

Elizabeth was taking her turn with their shared maid, and she was quite pleased with the results. Her hair sparkled with the jewels placed in it, the curls framing her face and the height just right. She had it on good authority that Mr. Darcy would be present at this dinner and she was determined to look her best. If they couldn't be together, she could still leave a lasting good impression.

At the very least, she could not have him in the world

thinking ill of her. And perhaps she might even encourage him to think kindly of her.

All the Bennets had been invited, and that was going to make favorable impressions difficult. Elizabeth loved her sisters, but the younger two were just that—young. They had not as yet learned to act with discretion and restraint. They often laughed loudly and long and dominated conversations at will, thinking wholly and completely only of themselves. It might be a trying evening indeed.

A maid appeared in the doorway. "A George Wickham to see you, miss."

Lydia ran by. "He's not here to see you."

Elizabeth heard her feet running down the hall and all the way down the stairs. Her loud "Mr. Wickham!" was clear from all over the house.

Jane stepped into their shared bedchamber. "You look more beautiful than ever." She stood behind Elizabeth at the mirror, both looking in the glass.

"As do you. You shall make Mr. Bingley even more in love with you."

Jane's face colored prettily. "I do think I could love him. He's such an amiable and good-natured sort of person."

"He is everything I would want for you so far. Take your time. Get to know him, despite what Mother might rush you to do."

"We have all the time in the world. It's lovely." Jane smiled the type of smile only someone as good as she could rightfully have. And then a slight trouble wrinkled the otherwise peaceful countenance. "And what about you? You aren't looking like you might steal the heart of every man in the room for Mr. Wickham, are you?"

Elizabeth shook her head. "No. He is unworthy of such effort. Though someone ought to tell Lydia." Their sister laughed overly loudly from downstairs. "What can he be thinking to play with our sister in such a way? He can't want anything more from her than he wanted from me?"

Jane eyed her sister in an overly knowing manner. "And what did he want from you?" She crossed her arms. "What have you been up to, Lizzy?"

Her cheeks colored before she could stop them. "Nothing overly untoward with the nefarious Mr. Wickham. We flirted. We were friendly." She shrugged. "And then I stopped wanting to."

Jane studied her a moment more and then shrugged as well. "Well, he is handsome. I trust him more with you than with our Lydia, I'm afraid."

"How so?"

"Well, your flirtations don't lead to stolen kisses and solitary rides. You are sensible enough not to lose your reputation over such a man. He can offer her nothing. He would never step up to marry her, and if he did, how would they live?"

Jane was so involved in her own suppositions on the plight of Lydia that she hopefully did not know recognize the guilt that overtook Lizzy. Sensible indeed. She was the least sensible person in regards to one Mr. Darcy. And she could not even regret it, not yet. In fact, she hoped for a few more stolen moments with him this evening.

"Lizzy, are you even listening to me?" Jane's face was flushed. She was obviously concerned.

"I hear you. I think we should talk to her, don't you? Tell Father?"

"Oh yes, definitely. Let's do so at once."

Lizzy followed her down to their father's study, but did not feel surprised when he downplayed their concerns and refused to talk to her. She draped an arm across Jane's shoulder after they left him. "At least tonight we know that nothing much could possibly come of their flirtations. There will be too many people about."

Lizzy knew she was talking about Lydia and Wickham, but she felt the words deflate her every hope to spend some time with Mr. Darcy. Of course he would be much sought after. Of course they would be under scrutiny, and of course she would not be able to steal any time with him. Where was his lovely Samson when she needed him?

The Bennet sisters were at last ready to go, all flustered and lovely in their dresses. Mrs. Bennet climbed in the very last, looking as lovely as any of them. She'd kept her beauty, and Lizzy could well understand why her father had married such a woman. He was noticeably absent.

They pulled away. "Where is Father?" Jane's face

revealed all the angst Lizzy, too, felt in thinking of the potential trouble with so many sisters to look out for and one chaperone.

"Oh, he's coming shortly. He wanted to finish a chapter of something." Mrs. Bennet waved her fingers as if it were of no consequence.

Perhaps it was of no consequence to their mother, but it would certainly affect Jane and Lizzy's evening, as they would be forced to look out for their sisters or subject the entire family to ridicule.

The Lucases' home was decorated in full splendor. Lights shone from every window. The sweet smell of flowers filled the air. People poured in the front door, and carriages lined the street. "It looks like people traveled to come," Lizzy said.

"The Lucases throw the best parties in the area. I do know she's expecting quite a few for dinner." Lydia grinned. "And a few of the regiment are coming only for the ball after."

"Is it to be a ball?" Jane turned to look out the window. "I thought it to be a dinner party with dancing and games?"

"Yes, but the dancing part has been much discussed, and Mrs. Lucas told the regiment they were welcome to come join in it. And so we shall get to dance with the officers after all."

Lydia's self-important flip of her head concerned Lizzy

even more than her words. "Please do try and control yourself. Our decorum matters."

Lydia turned away and whispered something to Kitty, who laughed so loudly, Lizzy was certain people heard from the street.

Jane placed a hand on her knee. "Please, Lydia. This isn't a game."

"Oh? And why not? Life can be enjoyed, you know. I plan on celebrating every last second of my life until I roll over into my coffin one day."

Mary placed a hand on her lips. "Lydia, really, to speak of dying in such a way."

"Oh, you're worse than Lizzy. Mary, just don't quote Fordyce's sermons and we shall all be relieved."

Jane placed a hand at her forehead. "Well, we have arrived. Please, everyone, remember you are a Bennet. It means something."

Lydia turned away without responding and allowed herself to be handed down first from the carriage. She and Kitty hurried in to the Lucases' arm in arm.

"I don't even know if they will remember to greet the Lucases." Lizzy sighed.

She felt someone's gaze. She turned, half hoping it would be Mr. Darcy, but two women she'd not met whispered together, eyeing her, and then hurried in the front door.

"What on earth?" Jane linked her arm with Lizzy's.

Mary followed behind with their mother, who was the most distracted Lizzy had ever seen her.

"I don't know what that was all about," Lizzy said.

"Perhaps they were already discussing something unpleasant and just happened to be looking in your direction."

But as more guests crowded closer to the entrance, people murmured together. They looked in her direction. Lizzy was definitely the subject of their conversation.

"I cannot fathom why I would be discussed."

As soon as they entered the door, Mr. Bingley stepped forward, all smiles. "How provident that you have arrived at almost the exact moment that we have arrived."

We? Lizzy's heart leapt in surprised.

Mr. Darcy stepped forward from the shadows, nodding at them both. His face was expressionless, but before he dipped his head, his eye sparkled at her in mischief.

And she didn't know if she could resist the sudden urge to immediately claim his arm.

Bingley offered his to Jane, which then left Mr. Darcy standing at her side. "May I escort you in?"

"Certainly." Her mouth fought against a full smile.

"Miss Elizabeth, if you smile at me, I don't know how I will resist any of your other charms," he murmured.

Her face heated immediately.

"Oh dear, and now I've made you even more irresistible." He looked away, but placed his other hand over the top of hers. "Come now. We must be decorous and beyond suspicion."

"Where is Samson when I need him?"

Mr. Darcy leaned back his head and laughed.

Her mouth dropped, and many in the area turned to look at them in surprise, and then began conversations anew.

"I believe I'm being discussed," she said.

"We certainly are right now. Who could have predicted a simple laugh to cause a stir?"

"No, before now, people were whispering and things." She moved closer to him.

He stood taller. "Perhaps we should not appear so intimate."

"Perhaps we should hurry in and find a corner to be lost in."

"Don't tempt me."

It was Lizzy's turn to laugh. The stress, combined with his nearness and overt flirting, were too much for her. The laugh bubbled out.

Everyone turned again, and the knowing looks from the ladies gave Lizzy pause. "I think they have been talking about us all along."

"What could they possibly have to talk about?" Mr. Darcy's eyes narrowed.

"Nothing I would like shared, I assure you."

They moved to the edge of the receiving room and a

footman announced their names. "Mr. Darcy and Miss Elizabeth Bennet."

Everyone in the room turned.

And Lizzy knew the source of their interest in her: the man standing at her side.

Chapter Sixteen

Lizzy's gaze moved about the room. Friends, neighbors, old gossips, all eyeing them as if they were a story about to unfold. "This is not good."

"What could they possibly be thinking? Act bored." Mr. Darcy suddenly relaxed all his features, his mouth turning into the sullen, prideful expression she'd seen upon first meeting him.

"Wow, that's effective. I don't think I can manage it."

"You must. Act as though you don't care what I do."

She laughed again.

"You are failing, Miss Elizabeth." He smiled. "But I can't say I would be altogether excited to see your dismissal of me." He did his own assessment of the room and then nodded. "Come. Let's hide in the library while we figure this out." His eyes shone with adventure, but she saw the wisdom in it, as well as the potential for some time alone with the man.

They nodded to all and sundry and then exited out the side door. "The library is this way." She led them down a hall. Everything got more quiet the further they walked away from the group, and then they slipped into an empty, mostly dark room. A stream of moonlight lit the back corner. They hurried to that corner and then moved slightly back into the dark.

Mr. Darcy pulled Elizabeth to him and her lips met his halfway. For a moment, she was lost in the magic of kissing and loving this incredible man. She held him, careful not to dishevel his hair, but doing everything she could with her mouth to claim him as hers. He seemed to do the same, their kisses at first a desperate longing. But after a time, he slowed and perused her mouth in what seemed to be a careful, long enjoyment. She all but melted at his feet, until much too soon, he stopped. "Elizabeth."

"Mmm."

"What is our plan?"

She laughed.

He sat in the nearest chair and pulled her into his lap. "Come now. We must avoid each other in public. We must not be seen together. That is the crux of it. For I cannot pretend disinterest, not when I'll be imagining your lips on mine." His eyebrows wiggled wickedly and she could do nothing but laugh.

"'Tis true. I believe you've found the solution. We should just not be together when others might notice. Do you think we can manage it as we walk back through that room and then separate ourselves?"

"We are made of the stuff that can do anything." He laughed to himself. "And we must. So we shall." He nodded. "Now come. This is a smallish party, and our absence will be noted."

With a sigh, she nodded as well, and then stood. He joined her, and soon they were standing side by side, ready to reenter the room from which they'd come.

Wickham met them in the hallway. "Well, well, well."

"Keep things to yourself." Darcy's clipped comment seemed to do the trick.

"I could say the same of you." His eyes held warning.

"What are you saying?" Darcy stepped closer to him and Elizabeth's fingers pressed into his arm.

"I'm saying that my business with your sister—"

"You have no business with Georgiana. Ever."

Wickham merely nodded and bowed in front of them. They walked by without another word.

Elizabeth's gaze bore into his. He wanted to tell her all. He wanted to confide his whole life to her. For she had become someone whose opinion he valued. In truth, he could use her assistance with his sister. He could use her advice. But now was not the time, and would there ever be a time? He was not free to encourage that relationship, not free to pursue Elizabeth. He sighed. But she was still waiting for him to respond.

"It is a tale I wish never to be repeated." He lowered his voice to a murmur. "He attempted to run off with my sister, to gain her fortune, convinced her they were in love." The pain of the memory tore another fissure in his heart just in its memory.

Elizabeth's soft gasp warmed his heart and he pulled her close into a hug. "It is a memory most difficult for me."

She melted into him and wrapped her hands around his back. "Then do not think of it. You owe me nothing." She rested her cheek against his cheek. "And that man is...She stiffened. "I wish I'd never known him."

"At least you will never be prey to something similar. He is a real danger." He pulled back and stared into her eyes, attempting to emphasize the seriousness of his words. "He has no scruples."

Though the whole conversation was unnerving, they had other things to manage at the moment. Elizabeth must convince all her friends and neighbors that she was not in love with Mr. Darcy. Her heart pounded against her chest. She'd have to convince herself first.

But as they stepped back inside, interested gazes and overly curious expressions met them. She felt her face heat. Something more drastic was needed. She knew that with

Darcy at her side, she could never be truly dismissive, nor could she look bored. "We shall have to manage this another way. Not a soul here will believe me to be resisting your charms."

His eyebrow raised, but he said nothing.

They stepped further into the room and then found their way to the back corner, where several spots were open on chairs and a sofa.

"We need to create a reason all these people might imagine we are together."

"Oh, I'm certain what they might be imagining." His eyes sparkled in the most enticing manner, and Elizabeth found herself sinking closer to him, not physically, but wholly, heartedly, emotionally. She sensed that if he stepped closer, she would feel that closeness, in her heart, in her head, in her very being. The idea was troubling, and possibly downright dangerous.

She cleared her throat. "Perhaps we are discussing my sister and your friend?" She nodded toward the two, obviously in love.

"We most certainly are. But what could they possibly need from the two of us?"

Jane laughed, her face blushing prettily. Bingley's face lit in delight.

Lizzy shook her head. "We would only mess up what appears to be perfection in a relationship."

Louder voices carried over to her. "I expect an announcement anytime," someone said. She smiled, but when she looked to grin at the person speaking, she seemed to be talking about Mr. Darcy. And, to Lizzy's shock, herself.

"No. I must do something drastic. I have to shun you . . . or cut you, or something. They are talking about an announcement. You will ruin me when you leave."

"Then I shall be as annoying as possible so that you might walk off in a huff."

Lizzy laughed and then placed fingers over her mouth. "Sorry. This will never do."

"But neither will your mother. You should be grateful that Bingley has a forgiving heart."

She stilled. "What do you mean?"

"She is one of the most nonsensical beings any of us has ever encountered. Come now, surely you have noticed. She has told all of your neighbors she herself expects an announcement any day."

"Surely you are exaggerating. And surely you cannot blame her. Our property is entailed . . ." Lizzy frowned. "I see. You hold my family in disdain."

"Do you expect me to rejoice in the inferiority of your connections? I'm not certain you realize what it means to be a Darcy."

"Well, I can assure you, this conversation is giving me a

wealth of information along those lines. And I am seeing quite clearly how being a Darcy could mean any number of things, not all positive."

"Since no proposals from me will be forthcoming, you need not concern yourself overly much."

"Oh never fear, Mr. Darcy. As handsome as you are, as enjoyable . . ." She swallowed back abrupt and delicious memories of just how enjoyable. "I'm quite certain you are the last person on earth I could ever be prevailed upon to marry." She stiffened, her breath coming in spurts, desperately attempting to hide her blush and trying an equal and desperate attempt to believe her own words.

She could not marry Darcy. She could not wish to marry Darcy. She could not be seen as hoping for such a thing. He would leave and her chances would be ruined everywhere. Even Darcy himself must believe she would not accept him.

His eyes flashed with hurt, but he nodded crisply, cleanly, one time and then indicated that she should leave. He leaned forward at the last minute and whispered, "Meet me in the library."

She whirled around and stomped away, only vaguely noticing that everyone in the room had ceased talking.

The last face to catch her glance before she flung open the doors and ran out into the street was the stricken and ghastly white face of her mother.

Lizzy dashed for the side door, nearly pushed through the frame, and exited out into the side garden. Her breath came in large gasps, filling her chest, but not quite satisfying an urgent need for air. Everything felt tight. Every movement hurt. She leaned forward, her hands on her knees, her head down, fighting the gray cloud encroaching on her vision, fighting the lightness of her head.

A swift break was necessary. It wasn't what she had planned, but providence stepped in, perhaps. For now, no one would think her pining away for Mr. Darcy. She'd essentially turned him down in a very public way. She gasped, a knife tearing through her chest. Was it possible anyone thought he'd proposed?

She gripped the fabric of her dress. There was a very real chance. Turning down a marriage proposal from the likes of Mr. Darcy would also ruin her.

She shook her head. "No. No. No." She planned her escape. She would run. Back to Longbourn and then . . . she didn't know what. Perhaps she'd visit her aunt and uncle in London. Or perhaps she'd hire out as a governess. Her breathing picked up. Her chest tightened. She was not prone to these forms of attacks. A part of her wondered if this is what Mama felt when talking of her flutterings and goings on. If it was, she felt a whole new sympathy for her. Voices approached and she picked up her skirts. The first thing to do would be to not speak to another person this evening.

"Miss Elizabeth."

She gasped.

Wickham stood at the gate. “I have a carriage.”

She nodded, ran to him, followed him out the gate, and climbed into his carriage.

Only when the door closed did she consider that they were alone, utterly unchaperoned in any way.

Chapter Seventeen

Darcy was left with a room full of silence and wide eyes directed at him. Though he felt like walking away, for Miss Elizabeth's sake, he gave a small smile and shrugged in the most humble manner possible. A few women smiled back and placed hands at their hearts. Then the rest, as one union of feeling, turned to each other and erupted in conversation. It was difficult to interpret whether they were favorably inclined toward Elizabeth or not.

Jane approached, and Darcy swallowed with relief. "Might I have this dance?" He held out his hand.

"After you so publicly were at odds with my sister?"

"It was all for show. I had to do it. People were talking of imminent attachments and her reputation was at stake."

"And it isn't now? Did you propose?"

He felt his face go ashen. "Of course not."

"And yet, she sounded as if she were declining a proposal."

"Were her words that audible?"

"They were."

People were paying close attention to them, and Jane's hand was still out stretched. "Then we must dance and act as though it is nothing."

"I agree. Or at least that we are unaffected. What is our story?"

"How about the truth?" He watched her, wondering just how much Elizabeth would have told her of the actual truth.

"Which is?" She studied him as he stood across from her, ready for their dance.

Others were listening in at this point. He spoke words he hoped would be repeated.

"You know I am promised elsewhere. Miss Elizabeth knows we have been nothing but friends, siblings now, come to think of it. I was helping plot a marriage proposal for her from friends in town and she became offended by my careless manner." He shrugged. "I assure you she will be pleased again in a short time. Once someone brings her a lemonade." He laughed.

"Well, of course. Anyone who has seen you together knows you have nothing but friendship in mind. And you are as honorable as any man. You would certainly keep your commitments elsewhere."

He nodded. "But I do have to say, I am pleased for my friend Bingley."

She then blushed prettily in response and looked up at him with such a glow of happiness, he could only be happy for his friend, happy indeed.

"You look so much like your sister when you allow your happiness to show." He couldn't quite keep the longing from his voice and had no idea what his face portrayed, but something about Jane made him wish to tell all. He turned from her then to dance with the other woman in their group, but her soft gasp told him that perhaps he had revealed himself.

Her knowing eyes when she returned to take his arm in the dance told him he had. But he did not admit further and did not speak much else for the remaining measures of their quadrille.

As the set was coming to a close, she stepped closer to him. "Thank you. I do so wish you were free to act on your heart." She curtsied low and then slipped away.

Her words shook him. Free to act on his heart. What was his heart dictating? Surely he had been listening to it? His mother governed matters of the heart, or so he thought. But of course, not in matters of romantic love. His mother had no place there. But he had believed he'd been acting in her best interest by obeying his aunt.

He tugged his cousin's letter out of his pocket and was about to find a quiet place to read it when his steps were blocked by several long skirts. The skirts were inhabited by young Mrs. Lucas and her daughters, and as the hostess, she had every right and obligation to approach him, and even expect that he remain dancing with her daughters. So he quietly pocketed the letter again and bowed. "Miss Charlotte Lucas, would you do me the honor of the next set?"

"Yes, thank you." She curtsied, and soon they were engrossed in a lively country dance. But her astute expression surprised him.

"You and my best friend are up to something."

He raised both eyebrows in genuine surprise. "Are we?"

"Yes, most certainly."

"I hope so, because the woman who stomped out of here looked as though she might never speak to me again."

"She did indeed. I'll give you that. She was authentically furious with you."

Could he blame her? He'd insulted her mother. But there was nothing for it. He'd had to. He looked around. "Has she returned?"

Her friend's face clouded with a hint of worry. "No, she hasn't."

Darcy's heart clenched suddenly. "Have you seen Wickham?"

Miss Lucas's eyes widened and then she shook her head. "No, I haven't. You know about Wickham?"

He shook his head. "If by know about him, you mean

do I know she was flirting with him? Yes. If by know about him, you mean he is not safe for most women? Also yes."

Her hands clenched in his. "What do you mean unsafe?"

"I am concerned enough that I feel we should leave the set to go in search of her."

She grabbed his hand, and they both left the dance floor just as they were about to turn and link arms with the other partner in their group of four. Miss Charlotte called over her shoulder, "Sorry. I'm having a bit of a ladies' mishap." She placed a hand at her mouth, as if she were going to giggle. As soon as she was turned back to him, she shook her head. "We need to hurry. She went out this way."

They rushed outside to an empty courtyard. "Do you suppose she went on foot?" Darcy strained his eyes into the darkness, but all he saw was a long empty road.

"I'd count on it. But let's ask around at the stables." She led him to her family's stables. "John. Could you tell me if you saw Miss Elizabeth?"

An older man with kindly eyes scratched his chin. "I'm not certain it was her. But young George Wickham had a carriage all ready to go out front—not sure where he came by it, mind. None of the horses came from here. And he did assist a young woman inside." He clucked, his disapproval of such a thing clear.

"If that was Miss Elizabeth, the highest discretion will be necessary."

"I will protect dear Miss Elizabeth. She was certainly not knowing what she was about, getting in a carriage with that man."

Darcy immediately liked John. He reached his hand out to clasp that of the older gentleman. "Thank you."

"Miss Elizabeth is the finest around."

Darcy nodded in agreement. "Do we know where they were headed? Or at least in which direction? Were they alone?"

John took off his straw hat and scratched his head a moment, then pointed down the lane. "They were headed that way, and as you know, the lane continues on for some distance before he would be able to turn off it. Depending on how fast he was going, you could catch them, or at least have some evidence of where they turned at the crossroads."

"I'll go at once!" Darcy turned about. "Is there a horse I could use? Already saddled?"

"Yes, right away." John ran toward the stables.

Miss Lucas began pacing. "What shall I do? No one can know. But am I to leave the life of my best friend in your hands? Yours alone?" Her eyes widened, and her desperate expression urged Darcy from his own planning and careful deliberations to realize she needed some comfort. At the very least they could not have a distraught Miss Lucas walking about the ball, causing suspicion.

He placed a hand on her shoulder. "I will do all that is in my power to bring back your best friend."

She studied his face and then looked deep into his eyes. After a moment, she nodded.

"Thank you. I know you will. And might I say, she is fortunate indeed."

"Let us pray you are correct."

John came running with a smart-looking animal.

"Oh good, he's brought Father's horse." Miss Lucas nodded.

"Thank you. Hopefully we will return in a short time."

She clutched his arm. "And if you don't? What shall I tell them? The family?"

"Tell her father the truth. Tell the others she had a headache." He gave her one last look of hope, and what he hoped was at least a small smile, and then he leapt on the horse and took off down the lane.

Chapter Eighteen

"Stop the carriage!" Elizabeth scowled at Wickham to hide the sudden panic she felt at being out of control of her situation, but she was certain the fear was evident on her face. Thankfully, her voice did not shake, however.

"Relax. I'll take you home. That's what you want, right? The way people were talking in there, you needed to leave when you did. And I was ready to take you. Providence. View it as such and relax. What happened?" He leaned back against the carriage bench, seemingly harmless, relaxed himself. So Elizabeth slowed her breathing a moment.

"It was terrible. Everyone was watching me, talking. And then I realized they were talking about Darcy and I."

Wickham clucked his tongue. "Word is that you two had a tryst in the library." His mouth twitched and his eyes danced with evil enjoyment.

"You did not!"

"I did. You wouldn't agree to my terms. People should know the truth about you."

Elizabeth's mouth opened in horror. "And what about the truth about you? Shouldn't they know what you did to Miss Georgiana?"

"Ah, so he did tell you. I'm sure his version is far worse than what actually happened. He cannot admit to himself that his sister might have actually sought me out, wanted to elope. No. He feels much better with the version he keeps close, that I abducted her."

Elizabeth's hands went cold as the carriage moved along at a brisk pace. "Much like I chose to go with you tonight?"

His eyes flashed in response, and for a moment, Elizabeth thought she saw real danger in his face. But then he smiled and picked a piece of lint off his pants. "More or less. Except that you hopped in my carriage willingly, looking for an escape. She hopped in hoping for a new life with me." His mouth pressed into a straight line. "Until her brother intervened."

The air had gone considerably more sour, and Elizabeth's arms lined with gooseflesh, her hairs standing on end.

"But did you love her? Or were you just after her dowry? She was so young!"

"Does it matter? She loved me. She was happy. I was willing to keep her happy the rest of her whole life. And before you pass some kind of judgement over there, don't tell me you aren't doing the same thing with Darcy right now." He crossed his arms.

She shook her head. "I'm not."

But at his look of incredulity, she stopped talking. He didn't deserve to know anything at all about Darcy. She knew she was sincere in her flirtation and honest with the man. She frowned. Had there been any truth in his complaints about her family? She peered out into the passing darkness in the carriage window. There had been. Which was why his comments stung. Would he be lowering himself so tremendously in aligning himself with her? She feared he would. It was for the better they were not to see one another again. At least that was what she would tell herself for many, many nights when she replayed the moments over again in her mind.

They came to the turn in the road at last. After this lane, they would go just a few more minutes and she would be home. "Thank you for rescuing me." She frowned. "How is it that you had a full carriage and horses at the ready tonight?"

A hint of uncertainty flashed across his face.

"Wickham. What were you going to do?"

He shook his head. "Nothing you need concern yourself with. Just be pleased I was there when you needed me." He rapped on the roof. "I could be much more for you if I'd been given the living I deserved. Imagine the happiness we could have, you and I together, if someone would stop withholding what is rightfully mine."

Elizabeth didn't know what to say about such personal delusion. "It is rather difficult to consider anything other than a small, insignificant flirtation when accepting the inevitable concerns of how one must live and exist in the world." She adjusted her skirts. "You have been a fun diversion, though. And I'm certain there are many avenues for you in the military, to earn your living . . ." She breathed out those few words, allowing the rest to fade away in the face of an increasingly furious Wickham. She swallowed. Venom lined his face in what was an awfully detrimental change to his previously handsome looks.

"I should be permitted to pursue whatever life I choose, with whomever I choose. That is the living that was promised to me, that is what Darcy stole, and what he will give back with every drop of the living he has remaining. It will be but a drop. He needn't be so selfish." Wickham leaned back, suddenly and alarmingly poised. He flicked another piece of lint off his pant leg. "With the proper motivation, I'm certain he can be reasoned with."

Elizabeth said nothing, but the now chilled atmosphere in the carriage lined her arms with more gooseflesh. She peered out the window, keeping her breathing steady. They were almost at the turnoff, and then just minutes from Longbourn. The coachmen was already slowing the horses to turn at the break in the road.

Wickham leaned back and closed his eyes. The carriage pulled to a stop, and he rapped on the ceiling, with eyes still closed, his cane raised above his head. And then the carriage began moving again, turning in the wrong direction.

"What are you doing?" Elizabeth leaned forward. "Wickham, where are we going?"

His mouth curled in insolence and evil. "Somewhere safe until we can be properly compensated."

She shook her head, gathered her skirts, and reached for the door. They were still moving slowly enough that she could fall onto the road outside.

But his hand gripped her forearm. "You won't be going anywhere."

She yanked it back, but he was surprisingly strong—and unyielding. She wrenched her arm this way and that, but it did nothing but rub the skin on her arm under the gloves. "You're hurting me," she called out.

But he just laughed. "You're hurting yourself. Sit tight and be still and you will be fine. I mean you no harm." He smirked, his face moving close to hers, so close she could smell the hint of onion on his breath. "On the contrary—you're my greatest asset, my ticket to the life I at last deserve."

"And what if I don't wish for such a life with you?"

He shrugged. "You are not necessary for this life, just in the acquiring of it. Once I receive my payment, you are free to go."

"Ruined? Abducted by you and then left to fend for myself? That's your plan?"

"You're welcome to stay, of course. I just sensed that you would find a partnership with me abhorrent. Beneath you?" He laughed to himself. "Not so above yourself now, are you? Come to grovel with the rest of us."

She at last pulled her arm free, but the carriage was moving at dangerously fast speeds and she didn't dare attempt a jump. "No thanks to you. And you're gravely mistaken. My father doesn't have the kind of funds you desire." Perhaps she could reason with him. "This is not going to work out as you are envisioning . . ."

But he just turned away.

She continued. "We have no money, sir. Please. Listen to me. No jewels, no hidden dowries, nothing. We have an estate that is entailed to our cousin. Our only hope of subsisting in the world is through marriage. And I refuse to marry for anything other than love. I don't care much for wealth, though like you, I would appreciate a living of some sort. I am the wrong person to abduct and hope for ransom." She would laugh if she thought the sound would come naturally from her tight throat. As it was, she imagined only sounds of strangled birds might come forth. "Listen to me."

He shook his head. "The only thing more frustrating than a woman who misuses her wiles is one who cannot see her own power. Such a waste." He clucked and then closed his eyes again.

She did not know what more to say to him. What would happen to her when he realized no one would pay? How would she ever make her way in the world? How could her family live respectfully? She realized she'd never marry now. Thoughts of Jane and Bingley brought sudden tears. He would soon withdraw his courtship. They would be left with nothing, at the mercy of Mr. Collins—and perhaps her best friend Charlotte Lucas. A sliver of hope warmed the smallest part of her heart. She could perhaps be a governess to Charlotte's children.

Chapter Nineteen

Sir Lucas's horse was a fine ride, thankfully, because Darcy had no way of knowing how far behind the carriage he had to race.

This is my fault. My fault. My fault.

With every stride, Darcy repeated the words to himself. Why hadn't he made Wickham's character known at every turn? Why had he allowed the man to associate in polite company? He could have him discharged, certainly.

He clenched the reins. One answer pounded through him.

Guilt.

Wickham deserved any repercussions coming to him. Darcy's brain knew it. But he couldn't erase his father's words, his father's care of Wickham. "Some are born to privilege and others rely on those with birthrights. Wickham is no less worthy."

Darcy's stomach clenched at the memory. How could his father have been so wrong about the man's character? And he'd left such an awesome burden of care on Darcy. Yes, Darcy had been born into privilege, and responsibility. And he had definitely attempted to deserve such. But Wickham had shown over and again that he was undeserving. And Darcy felt he had to clean up his messes simply because he allowed the man to exist.

And Elizabeth.

His heart bounded near out of his jacket in thinking her name. If anything happened to her . . . His teeth clenched tighter and he snapped the reins up against the horse's flank. "Hurry, old boy. She's worth a little extra tonight."

As if the horse sensed his care and the worthiness of the rescue, he burst forward even faster. "That's a good boy."

He lowered himself down onto the horse and tried to control his breathing. He would get to her before that cretin did one thing. His mind shuddered and he could think no further about what possible things Wickham might have done.

Elizabeth was a tough one, but she was vulnerable. She was tender. There was a softness and an innocence to her bold declarations that she wished for a flirtation. And that innocence, that new bud, was what he wished to preserve.

The road parted in front. He had to choose left or right. Without too much thinking, he veered off to the left. Longbourn was to the right.He supposed there was a tiny chance that he was actually simply taking Miss Elizabeth home, but Darcy doubted it almost as much as he doubted any other thing.

"Hiyah!" he shouted to the faithful animal beneath him. The horse responded with another burst of speed.

"You deserve your extra alfalfa tonight, there's a good boy." Darcy gripped the reins tighter, not out of desire to steady himself, but simply because he knew not what else to do with the added energy and angst.

Miss Elizabeth had to be well.

Or Darcy might not ever be again.

He rode for what felt like an eternity, when at last he saw a shadow moving in front of him. With squinted eyes, he could make out the outline of a carriage. And it was moving at dangerously high speeds.

It rocked side to side, the wheels hitting potholes and rivets in the road, bouncing and tilting precariously with each one.

Darcy's mind turned with possibilities. He must plan carefully how to go about the rescue. What if Wickham was armed?

But then a loud scream sounded in the air and Darcy lost all sense of reason. He called out in a raging kind of roar, his voice filling the night sky, and raced toward the carriage. As soon as he was close enough, he reached for the door and flung it open.

In the darkness, he could barely make out a hunched figure, or two figures.

"Darcy!" Elizabeth's panicked and alarmingly muffled voice spurred him to action. He reached for the carriage, clinging to the swinging door, leaned out, off his horse, and leapt inside. He reached for the back of a collar, gripped it as hard as he could, and flung the man backward.

Wickham teetered behind him and then lunged at his face.

Darcy faced his longtime foe, but he still hadn't seen Elizabeth's face. "Are you well?" he murmured behind him.

"Yes." Her voice sounded shaky, but he received comfort in hearing her.

"Stop the carriage." He raised himself to a hunched standing position, towering over Wickham. "Now, Wickham."

He looked as if he might not do as directed, but when Darcy took another step closer, he shrugged and then rapped on the ceiling.

The carriage began to slow.

"What is the meaning of this?"

Wickham's low laugh in response made Darcy's skin crawl.

Elizabeth shivered behind him.

His laugh subsided, and then he adjusted himself on his bench and flicked an imaginary piece of something off his pant leg. "Miss Elizabeth seemed in desperate need to escape. And so I offered her a ride."

Darcy frowned and glanced over her shoulder. "Did you willingly go with him?"

She stiffened. "I'm not sure I appreciate your tone of voice. But yes. He was supposed to take me home."

However unwise Darcy thought she was, he turned back to Wickham. "Get out of the carriage."

"Excuse me?"

"Get out. Now."

He leaned forward. "That's ridiculous. We are miles from anyone. I rented this equipage. You exit. Miss Elizabeth and I were getting on fine without you." His ugly smirk in the darkness begged to be punched, but Darcy resisted. Barely.

"I need to get Miss Elizabeth back to her home and you need to be as far away from her as possible. And you should know I will be reporting your behavior to your commanding officer. And everyone else I can think of."

Wickham clucked his tongue. "You will? And ruin the lady's reputation? No. You'll be keeping this as secret as our other adventure, won't you?"

"He most certainly will not. I'm not afraid to share with the world how unscrupulous you are." Elizabeth sat taller in her seat.

"Well, that's very noble of you in a sort of self-harming way, but I don't think you will."

Darcy sighed. "He's right. We can't risk your reputation."

"I don't mind . . ." She sucked in her breath. "But it would ruin Jane." She lowered her face in her hands for a moment. "I hate that you will get away with this, that people wouldn't just believe me that nothing happened and move on. What about your reputation?" Her head snapped back up. "It's all completely ridiculous."

Darcy wanted to pull her into his arms. But instead he held her gaze with his own, trying to pour understanding, strength, and tenderness into her. After a moment, her eyes welled up and she nodded.

"I agree. It's ridiculous. And that is why Wickham will walk home." Darcy stood. His large form towered over Wickham.

"I see you won't see reason. I can promise this: You will regret treating me with disdain. You will rue the day you crossed me."

"Leave now."

Wickham held up his hands. "Leaving." Then he kicked open the carriage door and exited out into the night.

Darcy followed. The driver peered down at him.

"There'll be additional compensation for your time. Please take us to Longbourn, and go by way of the back entrance by the stables."

"Yes, sir."

As soon as Darcy was back in the carriage, it began to move.

Elizabeth fell back against the seat and closed her eyes. "Praise be."

He moved to sit beside her and lifted her hand in his own. The eyes that met his were full of gratitude and such a raw vulnerability, he could not stop the hand that cupped her face, no sooner than he could stop his lips from finding hers.

As she melted into him, his arms encircling her in as protective a way as possible, his mouth tenderly caressed hers, trying to erase all the horrors of the past hour, hoping to infuse her with reassurance. Her hands ran up his arms and into his hair. The carriage rocked gently, and he willed it to take as long as possible to return to Longbourn, because he knew this would be the last time he held this remarkable woman in his arms.

Chapter Twenty

Lizzy could not get enough of Mr. Darcy. She held his head with one hand as though she could will it to stay. With her other hand, she clung to him like the lifeline he was, her fingers digging into his shoulder. He'd rescued her. He'd saved her at just the right moment. And his soft lips were so delicious that in that moment, she wanted to devour him. They pressed into hers, sending tremors through her core. Again and again, he moved his mouth over her, asking, responding, loving her.

She sucked in a breath. Loving? Where had her thoughts gone? She pulled away to stare into his eyes, but they were closed.

Slowly, his lids fluttered open, revealing the truth of her thoughts. Their darkness, the intensity there in his returning gaze, stole her breath again. Words would have ruined the moment. She leaned into him, insisting, asking for more. When she kissed him again, it was with the strength of her response to his unspoken declarations. She loved him too. She loved him with the fierceness of what could never be.

He groaned and then tilted her body in his arms, his fingers running through her hair, never releasing her mouth. "Elizabeth," he mumbled against it.

She smiled.

But he covered the smile with his mouth, his kiss pulling at her until her lips responded to his insistence.

At length, the carriage slowed, and the part of her not focused on kissing Mr. Darcy knew they must be approaching Longbourn. With a long reluctant pause and one last slow kiss, she pulled away just enough to say, "I think I'm home."

With a heart-tearing pain, she realized that was true in more ways than one. Mr. Darcy was her home. Her center, the place she most wanted to be in the world. A person. And in just a moment, she would leave his arms forever.

In a wild desperation, she clung to him. "Don't leave. Stay with me. I-I love you." She bit her lip, turning wide eyes to him.

She knew she'd made a mistake when he closed his eyes and leaned his head back, his features lined with pain. He shook his head.

And she pulled away. "I-I'm sorry. I don't know what came over me." She ran her hands down her skirts, attempting to straighten them. "How could I love you? I hardly know you." She could not meet his gaze again. In truth, she wished to hide under the covers of her bed for a few days, if not forever.

"Elizabeth."

She stopped fidgeting at the sound of her name and dared a peek at him.

The tenderness in his face had not changed. And his eyes had tears.

Her mouth dropped in amazement.

He rested his palm at the side of her face. "I would do anything so that you did not have to feel this pain."

She swallowed.

"But I am not free."

She nodded, a tear cascading over the edge of her eyes and down her cheek. She was embarrassed at admitting so much. But it was true. She felt her love for Mr. Darcy all throughout her whole self. She loved him, and she might love him forever.

The carriage stopped.

"I thank you. I would have been ruined." Her voice caught. "You have rescued my whole family."

"And no one can know. As far as anyone knows, you came straight home with a headache." He pushed open the door. "Wait one more moment, please."

He stepped out into the night air, which had taken a greater chill.

She peered out at him in the darkness. A bag of coins passed into the driver's hands.

How could she have been so incredibly stupid? To get in a carriage with Wickham, alone? And now Mr. Darcy was having to pay for her stupidity.

She knew she would spend many hours, days, probably weeks, maybe even the whole of her life dying of embarrassment over and over again when thinking of this night.

She stepped out of the carriage without waiting. "I'll just make my way in, then," she called over her shoulder as she hurried away.

"Miss Elizabeth, wait," he called after her, but she hurried faster.

Of course he caught up. His hand gently tugging on her wrist brought her right back into his arms.

"I cannot let you leave," he breathed into her hair. His hands moved up and down her back and then fisted her dress. "I cannot." He nuzzled her neck and she just clutched him, her face buried in his chest.

But at length, she stepped away. Wiping tears from her eyes, she stood taller. "Thank you. I should get inside now."

He nodded, holding on to her hand until her fingers slipped from his grasp.

Then she picked up her feet and ran toward the house, knowing she would never feel normal again.

Chapter Twenty-One

Darcy climbed back into the carriage and rode the whole way to Bingley's deep in thought. His new plan of action was formed before arriving at Netherfield. Wickham must be exposed. And then after a visit with his commanding officer, Darcy would return to his aunt's home and face whatever duty he must.

His heart closed. His face became a mask. And he knew that perhaps he was lucky to have tasted the joy of love for but a moment with a woman such as Elizabeth. Her eyes were so near in his thoughts. He could but close his own and there they were, mocking him, or loving him, or even disdaining him. He would love any of their expressions so long as they were directed at him. But they never would be again. For on the morrow, he would depart Netherfield. Nothing had happened that would change his plans. It could not.

Darcy arose extra early the next morning so as not to see anyone else before his departure. He left grateful notes for Bingley. But his heart was not at Netherfield. It resided at Longbourn, and he certainly would not be stopping there, for fear he would never leave.

His dreams had been plagued by Elizabeth's laugh, her wit, her smart and challenging quips. He was at a loss to rid her from his consciousness. For she was at every turn, in every thought, a part of his very existence at this point.

But it was to be expected. He'd just shared the kiss of all kisses with her the night before, felt her trembling frame in his arms.

The urgency to see her would fade.

At least he hoped as much, for he could not live with such an unrequited longing for the whole of his life.

He shook his head.

"Sir?" James, his valet, lowered his head with great deference. "Is there anything more you wanted?"

"No, we must be off. My thanks."

He nodded and directed the trunk to be placed atop Darcy's carriage.

The horses stamped their feet in readiness.

A gentle fog rolled across the surrounding fields as the first glow of morning lit the whole of his clandestine escape. The footman opened a carriage door. Darcy placed one foot on the bottom step.

And then he saw her.

A white flowing gown blowing in the wind on a figure on the hill, a woman who could only be Elizabeth. She raised a hand in the air.

He stared out at her for one long moment—maybe he could remember her thus, far and out of reach, instead of willing and loving in his arms.

He tipped his hat to her, though he doubted she could see such a small detail. Then he climbed into the carriage, rapped on the ceiling, and they were off.

He fought against the urge to look back. He was not a sap, after all. But just before they rounded the bend, he took a look. She was gone.

It was for the best.

Days later, he arrived at Rosings, the ancestral home of his aunt, Lady Catherine De Bourgh. With a mounting dread that pounded through his veins with every pained beating of his heart, he stepped out of the carriage to his aunt's outstretched hands.

"Oh, my dear nephew. It is good to see you home at last where you belong." She squeezed his hands with a fierceness not born of love, but of need—of desperate, grasping need.

The strength with which her old frame held him was remarkable, almost as strong as the force of her will over him.

But there was nothing for it. Whether he resisted being controlled by such a woman or not, he could no sooner go against his mother's dying wishes than break the heart of his cousin.

He regained his hands and then bowed with deference. "Aunt, you look well. I assume you are in good health?"

"I am indeed now that you have arrived, and not a moment too soon. You will greatly revive your cousin's constitution. She awaits in the drawing room."

He groaned within himself. "Surely, Aunt, you would prefer I freshen up? Revive myself from the journey?"

A troubled cloud crossed her face, but she recovered. "Certainly. Anne should like a respite herself, I imagine. All that fresh air on the veranda tired her this morning, I'm afraid."

Darcy nodded. "Then we shall meet for repast?"

"Yes, thank you, nephew. Your mother would be proud of the man you have become, and for the steps you are taking to make all our wishes come true."

He looked away from her searching and calculating eyes. It was one thing to do his duty, and quite another to be hounded and pestered into it. She was enough to make him want to turn his back on Rosings forever. The sooner he left his aunt's presence, the better.

After his bath and a fresh change of clothes, he felt much revived. He focused on his mother's words. The memory was only slightly faded. She had called him into her room, just hours before she would leave Earth forever. He'd cradled her hand in his own, knowing it would be the last time he saw her, but not wanting it to be so. He'd spoken of other things, the meadow in the spring, how he would return to see her, the beauty of her sitting room with the sun streaming in, the books she loved.

She listened, her soft eyes welling with tears, until she squeezed his hand. "Fitzwilliam."

He paused and leaned closer to hear her soft, weak voice.

"I love you, my son. Take care of your sister. And remember Anne. She is in great need of your rescue." Her breaths had become shallow, and she paused to catch enough of one to continue. "You are the only one who can save her." She'd begun mumbling then, sounds incomprehensible to him.

He stayed and listened until she was again quiet, eyes closed, at peace. And then he'd kissed her brow. "I love you, Mother. I shall do my duty by Anne." When he was on the other side of her bedroom door, once again in the hall, a cold, sterile loneliness permeated the air around him.

He would be orphaned. It had felt as though all of Derbyshire rested on his shoulders starting in that moment. Pemberley certainly did, as well as the well-being of his beloved sister Georgiana, and now his cousin Anne.

The memories did not bring greater peace or well-being to himself in that moment, standing in his rooms at Rosings Park, but they did fortify him with the strength of desire to assist his cousin despite the loathsome manner in which his aunt behaved.

A glance out his window showed Anne being wheeled about in a chair of sorts by the servants. She was bundled to such a degree that Darcy was surprised the fresh air reached her at all. And they stuck to the shade. In truth, she might be chilly in the early morning air with no sun on her face.

He adjusted his gloves, slipped on his outerwear with the help of his valet, and made his way outside.

He steeled himself in his approach. After bowing in front of the bundle of linens and hearing some sort of muffled reply, he nodded to the servants. "I will continue on the walk from here. If we could have one maid following at a discreet distance, that should suffice."

The servants seemed grateful to depart. And when they were at last and finally alone, Darcy knelt down in front of his cousin. "Might I relieve you of some of your wrappings?"

"Please." Her voice sounded stronger than he expected.

She reached for the scarves encircling her face and tugged to get him started.

What he saw after the unveiling made him smile.

She was lovely.

Her striking blue eyes pierced him with a beauty that he was not expecting. "Hello there, my cousin Anne. And how are you this morning?"

She smiled at him from deep within the folds of her

many wrappings. "I shall be much better when most of this is stripped off me. Could you please be of further assistance?"

He chuckled at her frustration, though he shouldn't. Hers wasn't a momentary roadblock to happiness, but a lifetime of a controlling mother. Her present state was so indicative of her treatment and isolation at home. She was in desperate need indeed. He made a quick work of the wrappings, and at last Miss Anne was left with a smart hat, a normal jacket of sorts, and a warm muff.

"Ah, now that I can breathe and see you properly, thank you for coming, Fitzwilliam."

"I see I've come not a moment too soon." He smiled.

"'Tis true. But I do not expect you to be trapped here like me. I'll just be grateful for the days you can spend the time." She shifted in her seat. "Would you mind if I leaned on your arm a bit for our walk?"

"Most certainly." He hid his surprise at her request. He was under the impression that she was bound to a chair, that walking was no longer possible.

She winked at him. "I'm much better off than anyone thinks."

His assists in rising from the chair were gratefully received. But soon, she was standing steadily with two hands wrapped around his arm, and seemed to be doing famously.

"This is much better, thank you. Shall we?" She indicated with her chin that she would like to walk toward the water.

"I should be honored."

They began at a slow pace, but Anne seemed to manage well enough. After only a short time, with the new color in her cheeks, she was actually quite fetching. Surely there were many men who would be only too happy to marry her. Perhaps it would not need to be him.

"Tell me, Darcy, how have you been passing your time?"

His thoughts immediately went to Elizabeth, of course. But he squelched those almost as quickly as they had come. "I've been supporting Bingley in a most advantageous lease of land. He's to be gentry, more than his merchant upbringing, and he's quite thrilled about such a prospect."

"As he should be. From what I hear, his parents were most diligent in providing such a living for him and his sisters."

"They were indeed. It makes me remember my duties." He shrugged and strained a bit against the tightness of his collar. "I am more motivated to ensure the estate continues to grow and not shrink in the coming years. I owe my posterity."

"You, of all people, are the most trustworthy of such a legacy. Pemberley is in good hands." She paused, and Darcy could sense the import of what she was about to say. "And the influx of Rosings Park would significantly aid in those aspirations, surely."

He bit back a sigh. “Yes, most certainly. Is it time we discuss what our mothers schemed all those years ago?”

“I know that we are but acquaintances, but I would like to be a friend to you, to be a partner. I don’t require much, even if my mother insists otherwise.” She lifted a handkerchief to her mouth. “But, Fitzwilliam, you deserve an heir.”

Astounded at the immediate personal nature of their conversation, he sucked in a breath.

“And I am unsure I have the health to survive such a thing.” She walked along with her gaze forward even though he studied the side of her face. “But walking with you helps.”

“You are remarkably strong for one supposedly bed or chair ridden.”

Her mouth wiggled in a small smile. “I walk the halls at night after Mother is in bed to prevent her apoplexy at seeing me up and about on my own.”

A great mountain of irritation rose in his chest. “Should I talk to her? This seems a most ridiculous mode of survival.”

“It is most ridiculous. But at the same time, I find it difficult to fault her. She is my mother, after all, and all she does is in response to a great love for me.”

“Certainly. And perhaps some sense of control she finds it difficult to relinquish.”

“Perhaps.” Anne lifted a shoulder and seemed to want to talk of other things.

"Tell me about spring here at Rosings Park. I think I shall pass the season with you and Aunt."

"I'm so happy to hear it. We shall make sense of our situation, cousin. Let us have a goal to make our decisions by the end of your time here?" She turned to him, and the hint of pain in her eyes found a way to latch on to his heart in a painful sort of injury. He wished to do what he could to heal that hurt, to assuage her pain, and to make things right in her life. Surely, she could improve her health this spring with him to assist. Sun and walks would do the trick. If he could but get her to a state where he knew she would survive, that she could have children, then certainly they could get along well enough.

Immediately, thoughts of Elizabeth disrupted amenable thoughts of marriage to anyone else, platonic or otherwise. Hopefully by the end of spring, thoughts of her would simply be a pleasant memory and not so preventative of happiness elsewhere. But as her eyes mocked him in his thoughts, sparkling with the wit of a delicious word battle, he began to wonder if such a thing would ever be possible. Could he really forget the intensity of his feelings toward her? And how could he live the rest of his life pining for a woman out of reach?

Questions he may never answer plagued him for the rest of their walk. Even though he discovered that Anne had a lovely laugh and that her humor was intact, that she was secretly reading books his aunt disapproved of, even with an increasingly engaging woman at his side, he battled questions about Miss Elizabeth. *Give it time*, he told himself. But even as he thought the words, he doubted their veracity.

Chapter Twenty-Two

Elizabeth prepared herself for the day, hoping that Mr. Darcy would stop by. Jane entered their room, humming and smiling to herself. "Bingley is coming this morning, and we wish to walk to Meryton. Perhaps you would join us?"

"Of course. I would do anything to assist you two. I've never seen a happier duo. If Mr. Darcy comes, it will be even easier."

Jane stopped and turned slowly. "I think Mr. Darcy left at dawn."

Elizabeth's chest tightened and her next breath came in louder than she would have liked, more like a strangled cry than an actual breath. "How can you know that?"

"He told me last night. Bingley said he was determined to leave."

Elizabeth's chest loosened somewhat. Surely his plans

would have changed now, now that they had shared such a kiss, such a moment. He hadn't said as much; in fact, he'd been pretty certain that they could never be, as usual. But after a whole evening dreaming of him and remembering the look of love in his face, she just couldn't believe it. How could a man live so contrary to his own happiness? Why and how could a person do such a thing?

She readied herself with extra care, certain he would arrive, certain he would make the ultimate choice of happiness for them all. Surely he was more free to make such choices than she. What could stand in his way once he made his mind to choose happiness? To choose love? She shook her head. No. He would come.

By the time the servant announced Mr. Bingley, Elizabeth was so certain Darcy would follow that she ran to the door to meet him.

Bingley bowed over her hand and said, "A pleasure as always to see you, Miss Elizabeth. You are looking well."

"Thank you." Her curtsy was quick and distracted as she looked over and around his shoulder.

"Is Mr. Darcy tying up the horses?"

His expression clouded. "Oh no, miss, I'm sorry. He sends his regards. But he left at first light this morning. Family duties called him to the North."

"Oh, I see." She felt her mouth smile as she turned from him.

Jane entered the receiving area, obviously tired of her

perch in the front room. She and Bingley soon became lost in each other.

But for Elizabeth, the world had lost all color.

All she wanted to do was return to her bed.

"Hill!" Her mother's shrill call for their servant changed her mind immediately.

"You will join us on our walk?" Jane's sweet reminder filled her heart with relief.

"I'd like nothing more. Let me fetch my bonnet."

She joined them at a distance, and it ended up being the best remedy for her immediate loneliness. Loving and then losing felt worse than having never loved. She was proof of such a thing, and wished not to be. For after knowing the companionship of Darcy, feeling his caring, loving him, she would forever miss such a connection. She would miss him. And she didn't know how she would ever feel whole again.

She kicked at a rock.

Jane's joyful laugh carried to her. Their heads were bent together, talking of everything and nothing, Elizabeth assumed, as people in love. And she could at least find solace in such a relationship.

Their mother had been much calmer of late with the idea that the rest of her daughters would be cared for by such a marriage. She had sat calmly at breakfast the other morning with a pleased smile and complimented Mary.

Elizabeth was happy for them all and should be relieved herself to be taken care of. But as Darcy's smile entered her thoughts at any moment, she knew it would take a long time. And suddenly the walk to Meryton, her life at Longbourn, and their friends all seemed small and closed in, where they had just days ago felt like enough.

Even Charlotte had left her. Granted, she'd planned to marry. But it felt like such a poignant loss.

She stopped by the Lucases' once they had arrived in town. Jane and Bingley joined a group of the officers in a promenade down the main street.

Lizzy kissed Mrs. Lucas's cheek. "And what news do you have of Charlotte?"

"I'm so happy you stopped by. This letter came this morning and there's a page for you." She opened up the paper, written on all sides, using every possible open space, and lifted a folded sheet with *"Lizzy"* written in Charlotte's careful scroll.

She clutched it to her heart. "Excuse me a moment." She moved to a sofa and opened the paper as though it held great treasure.

"My Dearest Lizzy," Charlotte began.

Tears filled Elizabeth's eyes. How she missed her friend as she imagined all the things she would tell her of Mr. Darcy. She blinked back the blurry image and read a delightfully newsy letter where Lizzy was pleased, indeed, at Charlotte's situation. She seemed happy. And at the end of the letter, she implored Elizabeth to come visit.

"The only thing I lack in my new situation is you. Come,

Lizzy, come at your earliest convenience. Come with my father and sister. Just come. We have space and more for you. And I do believe you will enjoy the walks and the beauty here almost as much as that of Longbourn."

Lizzy scoffed, and then folded the letter. "Mrs. Lucas?"

She looked up from her needlepoint, and Elizabeth continued. "Charlotte says Sir Lucas is traveling to see her. Might I join them?"

Mrs. Lucas clapped her hands. "I admit to being privy of the invitation and I'm so pleased you are willing. For our youngest is afraid to go if you are not joining."

Lizzy laughed. "Why should she be afraid?"

"From all we've heard of the infamous Lady Catherine De Bourgh, she says you are the only one to be half-strong enough to face up to such a woman."

Lizzy shook her head. "And why should we have to face up to her? I'm sure it will all be lovely. We have manners to fall back upon, do we not? And surely Lady Catherine will also be lovely."

Mrs. Lucas nodded. "Too true. Such a sensible woman. I'm so happy you will be joining them, as I said. Now let's just hope your mother can spare you. They shall be leaving in a week's time, if that is convenient?"

"Yes, quite. The earlier, the better, I'm sure."

Chapter Twenty-Three

Weeks passed, and Anne was getting stronger by the hour. Monday morning had dawned, and they sat at breakfast together. She held up the paper from town and read out the gossip while Darcy contemplated his food. He also thought more than once on Elizabeth, if he were being honest. He was always contemplating Elizabeth. But that morning, watching Anne with energy and a sparkle in her eyes, listening to her laugh, he decided that sharing a life with such a pleasant soul would not be so bad.

As long as he wasn't constantly reminded of Elizabeth.

He chuckled at something Anne said. "Wait, please read that again, cousin. Did I hear you correctly?"

"I'm afraid you did. Someone has taken out an advertisement in search of a wife." She cleared her throat. "Seeking woman of great kindness. She must speak with deference in mild tones and must approve of me most of the time. A woman who adores children would be helpful in that we will not have a nursemaid nor help in the nursery."

"He doesn't want a wife. He needs someone to look out for his children." Darcy laughed.

But Anne's smile faded. "I can't say that I would complain. Children would be such a blessing."

Darcy reached out a hand to take hers. "And you're getting stronger every day."

Aunt Catherine joined them at that moment, Darcy holding Anne's hand, staring meaningfully into her eyes.

"And why shouldn't she be getting stronger? You have revived her, dear nephew. It is all she needs to make a full recovery. Your mother and I always knew." She joined them at the table, her servants madly filling a plate.

She eyed the offerings and sniffed. "The eggs look soggy. Could you please get me a lighter selection?"

"Yes, my lady." The footman bowed and removed her plate, in search of fluffier eggs, Darcy presumed.

Her eyes turned calculating as she studied Anne. "You are looking consumptive, though, my dear. Perhaps you should take to your rooms and the enclosed air for a few days. We can't have Darcy weakening you right when we had such hopes of improvement."

Anne started shaking her head.

But Lady Catherine quelled her with a look.

Darcy glanced from one to the other, wondering what

on earth this woman had over her grown daughter to make her cow in such a way.

"Aunt, I should like to spend more time out of doors with Anne today."

"You'd have her fall ill."

"It is my opinion that she will only become well by doing so. She's much improved from when I first arrived. The color in her cheeks could be from healthy exertion."

She raised her chin. "This is a false high, a moment where she is rallying to greet you, but once she becomes overly exhausted, it will take its toll. You will see."

Darcy studied her face, but then turned to Anne. "Would you like to go for a walk this morning?"

She glanced at her mother and then away. "I . . ." She bowed her head. "I do believe I should take to my rooms for a day or two. And then we shall be up and about again."

She did not meet his gaze, and he felt powerless to help. "Perhaps I could bring in some of the wildflowers in the back fields to cheer your rooms, then?"

Lady Catherine could not look more pleased, rising in her seat as though peacock feathers sprouted behind her. "Excellent notion, Fitzwilliam."

Anne lifted a grateful expression in his direction, but it was fleeting as she turned her attention immediately back down to her plate.

Lady Catherine reigned over the rest of breakfast, filling the room with all manner of her pontifications on any number of topics. But Darcy's mind was whirring with a stronger awareness of Anne's need to be free of her mother. He could not invite her to visit Pemberley alone. Surely her mother would join her. And then Darcy would be submitted to her insufferable insistence on the best manner in which to fund his estate. Georgiana would need to be spared, at the very least.

He rubbed a hand over his face.

"Are you well, nephew?" His aunt's scrutiny was more oppressive than he could stomach at the moment.

He wiped his mouth and stood. "I am well, yes. I shall make use of the extensive grounds here at Rosings to go for a ride. I do believe my horse is in need of some attention."

"Of course." She waved her fingers, and servants came to clear all their plates.

He bowed to them both and turned on his heel to leave the room posthaste. Perhaps his escape was an abandonment, but he could no longer abide the room and the cowering weakness of Anne's response. And something did not make sense to him. What was the cause of her silent rebellion that could be squelched at a glance?

His thoughts carried him all the way to the stables. The servants seemed to already have been advised to his plans. His horse was saddled and ready for him at the entrance.

"Thank you." He nodded to the stable hand. Then he leapt up on the back his magnificent animal and turned from Rosings, down the lane and away from the lands and influence of his aunt.

After keeping Samson from going too swiftly down narrow lanes, and seeing no one for miles, he at last gave the horse his head and leaned forward as the wind rushed past him, and they picked up speed. Escape. He needed to be as far away as possible. He couldn't explain it. His heart pounded through his chest. His hands gripped the reins tighter than necessary. His thighs squeezed at the flank. He could not endure another moment in his aunt's presence, and yet he was considering tying himself to her forever? Linking Pemberley and Rosings Park for all time? Seeing Anne's obedient face told him just how much influence her mother had on her.

Yes, she needed assistance.

But could he provide what she needed? Could he doom himself to the same life existence? If his reaction to breakfast were any indication, no, he could not. Not without destroying any hope of a peaceful life.

Naturally, the woman could be quelled. He hoped. But at what cost to his own peace of mind? What lengths would need to be taken to limit her influence? Hide her away? Put her in a dowager cottage without a carriage? He could hardly imprison his aunt. And were his thoughts really merited? She was an older woman trying to do her best by her daughter, was she not?

It was not like him to react so strongly, nor for his emotions to take such reign. What had come over him?

The longer he rode, the more his mind was able to calm his emotions until, miles later, very far from any sight of Rosings Park, he saw the very core of his concern. And it had nothing to do with Miss Anne at all.

Elizabeth.

As he saw hints of what his life was bound to be like if he continued to do his duty and married Anne, he felt that much further from his true heart's desire, which was to ride this same horse up to Longbourn, scoop her up in front of him, and then ride off again toward Pemberley.

He smiled at the thought and allowed a bit of fantastical imaginings. He could almost feel her in his arms, her hair tickling his face as she leaned back against him, her form molding to his in the perfect fit. He knew she was made for such a ride with him because he'd held her there before. He could almost smell the lemons and rosemary or hints of lavender that she was known to wear. Her hair was soft. Her hands held his arms at her side. And she laughed. He'd never met a woman who faced situations without great amounts of trepidation or worry. She seemed to welcome life with whatever it would bring.

He was so lost in his imaginings that he did not notice an approaching carriage until it was too late to avoid. Every possible turnoff was well behind him. Remembering his first encounter with Miss Elizabeth, instead of racing past at his current speed, he moved to the side and stopped to wait for the carriage to pass him.

They approached, avoiding potholes in an expert manner. Darcy was quite impressed with the driver. But the equipage stopped, the man pulling hard on the reins. "Whoa, there. Whoa, ladies." He dipped his head and touched his hat to Darcy.

Darcy responded with the same. "What can I do for you, sir?"

A female gasp of surprise from inside the carriage drew his attention. "Who goes there?" he asked.

The window covering moved and revealed someone who looked vaguely familiar, a young miss. "It's Mr. Darcy!" she cried out. Then she put a hand over her mouth. "Beg your pardon, I'm surprised, that is all."

Then Sir Lucas opened the door. "What a boon to see you here." He held out his hand and shook from the first step on the carriage. "I could use a bit of a stretch. Come, ladies. I'm sure the air will do you good." He reached a hand out to help his daughter. "I'm not certain you have yet been introduced to my youngest. This is Miss Maria Lucas."

She bobbed a nervous curtsy.

"And you remember Miss Elizabeth." He reached a hand back.

Darcy's heart felt like it stopped and then began again in the matter of one breath, so startling to him that it brought a cough at the back of his throat, which he attempted unsuccessfully to ignore. Pounding his chest, with watering eyes, he dismounted and hurried to reach a hand out to help Miss Elizabeth down from the carriage.

"I do remember." His outstretched hand reached into the darkness of the carriage. He wondered if she would take it. He wondered if she would ever forgive him for simply leaving. Without word, without any sort of preparation, he had left Netherfield. He winced at the awkwardness for her and hoped there had been no pain.

But of course there had.

And the attempted stoicism she exhibited told of the pain. Her trembling lip, her initial attempt to avoid his gaze, and then meeting it head on with a soft tenderness that stole his breath.

"Oh my dear," he mumbled. "How sorry I am."

She sniffed and her expression cleared. "I'm not certain you are."

She pushed past his offered hand and dismounted on her own. But as soon as she did, she turned, an apology in her eyes. "It's just too much."

He nodded, briefly. "Yes."

When they faced a rather curious-looking pair of Lucases, they both seemed in control of their faculties.

"And to what do I owe this great pleasure in seeing you here?" Darcy looked from one to the other, more than mildly curious, but keeping his tone light.

Miss Elizabeth was the one to answer. "We are come to

visit Miss Charlotte, newly Collins. You might remember tales of Mr. Collins?" Her eyes twinkled for a brief moment.

"Ah yes, I do remember. And he lives here? I'd forgotten."

"His property abuts Rosings Park, if you know that estate."

"I do indeed. You are not far. Though by carriage, it will still take you the better part of the morning to arrive."

His arms ached to pull Elizabeth up in front of him on the horse. She watched him with eyes that might never let him go, though she tried not to. He could tell by the amount of times she looked away; but shortly after, her gaze returned to him.

Chapter Twenty-Four

Elizabeth needed to run. She needed to get as far away from Mr. Darcy as she possibly could, and quickly.

But no one was moving.

Sir Lucas looked as though he wished to discuss all things at great length with Mr. Darcy from the middle of the road. His daughter was no better. Her doe eyes and blinking eyelashes were completely lost on Mr. Darcy, but Elizabeth knew they would not let up anytime soon. And in the meantime, she was at great risk of melting into the dirt of the road or throwing herself at him, begging for a return to the strong arms that held her atop that very horse before.

She was a complete ninny and she didn't know what to do with herself. A slight sway on her feet and Darcy leapt forward with his arm outstretched. "Are you unwell?"

"I-I don't know." She clutched at his arm and dipped

her head. The dark spots cleared. "I have never experienced anything like that." She would never admit to anyone that she'd almost swooned. That was a supremely un-Elizabeth-like thing to do. Perhaps Kitty or Lydia or even her mother, with her fits and vapors, but she, Elizabeth, had never, nor thought she'd ever be in need of a man's arm to support her through a dizzy spell.

"Forgive me," she mumbled.

"I admit to being pleased for an excuse to offer you my arm." He turned so that only she could see his mouth moving. "Pray, might we walk a moment while the others rest?"

"I don't see how that is possible since you are much in demand for conversation." She turned meaningful eyes in Sir Lucas's direction. The man seemed to be waiting for a response.

"Too true." He held out his other arm for Miss Maria. "Perhaps we might converse while we walk a moment, if you could do my horse the honors?"

"Oh certainly." Sir Lucas tied the horse to the others at the carriage, and they began a slow meandering pace down the lane.

No one said anything for several minutes. Sir Lucas kept a watchful, deferential eye on Mr. Darcy. Maria fidgeted with the ribbons on her dress. And Elizabeth refused to meet Mr. Darcy's gaze, which he kept focused on her for many moments. All of it felt so ridiculous to her that after but a few steps, she sighed. "Do you know? I think I would rather rest in the carriage, if you don't mind. I haven't eaten well today, and I think the long days of travel are affecting me more than I would expect."

Her heart pounded at Darcy's nearness and could hardly bear the burden of knowing he did not wish to be with her. The man she most wanted in the world, and he'd left. He'd refused to give them a chance. He'd kissed her mercilessly, claiming her as his, branding her with his own addictive offering and then drawing away the moment she knew she couldn't survive without him. The more she thought about his behavior, the angrier she became. Without so much as a further glance in his direction, she whirled on her feet and marched back toward the carriage.

She expected to be left alone, but within seconds, a hand wrapped around her forearm. "Elizabeth." Darcy's low voice in her ear sent gooseflesh down her back.

She paused her steps and refused to turn to face him. "You have to leave me be."

"Please. A moment?"

She shook her head.

"I believe you deserve my apology, an explanation at the very least . . ." His pleading tone tempted her to acquiesce, but she fueled her discontent with memories of his disdainful arrival the first day they met, with mud sliding down her face.

"I do deserve your apology. I deserve much more where

you are concerned. But I do not care to hear it. I think it best if you just give me space to forget you." She glanced over her shoulder and regretted immediately the view of his pain-filled expression. "Please. Let me forget you."

He stared into her eyes for what felt like the longest, most torturous moments of her life and then nodded, once. "I shall leave you in peace."

She dipped her head in gratitude and then picked up her pace and ran back to the carriage, climbed into the furthest corner, and allowed the tears to flow.

Why, oh why, did Darcy have to be here of all places? She'd come to distract herself from the constant memory of him plaguing her peace. She'd come to leave him behind.

Sounds of horse hooves riding away brought her no sense of satisfaction. He'd left again. Even though she'd told him to, the departure hurt almost as much as the initial news that he'd left the first time. She supported her forehead in her hands. How was one to get over such a man? How was one to feel whole when a part of her rode away on that horse just now?

A few moments later, a curious-looking Sir Lucas and a relieved Maria rejoined her in the carriage. The carriage began to move again, and after a moment, Sir Lucas cleared his throat. "You and Mr. Darcy seem to have a history of sorts."

He waited for her to elaborate, but all she did was shrug. "Not really. As you know, his friend Mr. Bingley spends considerable time with my sister Jane, and Darcy and I were therefore needed often at their side."

He nodded and did not look convinced, but Elizabeth had no need to convince him.

Darcy was correct; after a couple more hours, they turned onto a lane that would at last lead them to the Collinses' residence. On their left, a well-manicured sprawling estate, lined with a low stone wall, full of old trees and grassy knolls, beckoned to her. It looked to have the best walking nooks and open spaces as well. She longed to run out across the grass and never stop.

Sir Lucas peered out the window next to her. "I do believe that is the estate of the esteemed Lady Catherine De Bourgh."

"We have certainly heard much about it. I wonder what it will be like to make her acquaintance," Elizabeth said.

"Oh, you don't think we shall have to speak to her, do you?" Maria asked, her voice quivering.

Elizabeth laughed. "I'd imagine so. It would not do for our Charlotte's family to appear as simpletons, would it? We must present our best foot forward, mustn't we?"

Her face paled, but she nodded. "I shall try."

Sir Lucas patted her hand. "You will do famously. And I'm certain you will enjoy the grounds with your sister and Elizabeth. We shall find much to divert ourselves, I'm sure."

Lizzy nodded. She was most looking forward to the quiet wisdom of her friend. Perhaps she could assist in her efforts to let go of the thoughts that kept spiraling around in her brain. What if she had been more kind to Darcy? What if she'd told him how she felt before the ridiculously vulnerable declaration of love? Too many what-ifs, with no answers. She had no understanding of his situation or what made him unavailable. But if he knew he was so unavailable, he should have resisted her in every way.

A quiet voice told her she should have done the same.

But there was nothing for it. What's done was done. All she could do now was shelter and protect what was left of her heart.

She told herself she was happy to send Darcy away.

But nagging thoughts asked questions. What was he about to tell her? Perhaps she would like to know what kept him so bound?

She shook her head.

Sir Lucas turned to her with more questions in his expression, but said nothing. She looked out the window.

A lone figure of a woman walked across the great expanse of green. She was dressed in finery and was alone. Her pace was slow at first. She seemed almost to struggle with every step. The wind whipped her hair. It blew against her dress, causing it to billow out around her. But she pressed on. Lizzy watched with growing fascination. Each step seemed almost a personal battle against the elements. Why was she alone? Where was she going?

They passed by, and Elizabeth watched out behind them

as long as she could. At the last moment, the woman began to run. She held her arms out at her sides as if enjoying the pace and ran into the wind.

The carriage pulled out of sight. But Lizzy was left with a supreme sense of longing. She would have leapt from the carriage to join the woman if it would have been even remotely acceptable.

At length, with the estate of Rosings still at their left, they stopped in front of a lovely home. A white fence in front lined the quaint property. Chickens clucked in the back. Two garden areas were overflowing with blooms. Everything was well cared for and pleasing to see. Charlotte's hand was everywhere Lizzy looked. And then off to the right, an old tree with thick branches hosted a single swing.

Her throat constricted, remembering her farewell to Charlotte at a similar swing in front of her own home. Charlotte had said, "Don't mock me, Lizzy. I am tired of being a burden to my family."

Lizzy's breath caught at the memory. She, too, would be a burden to her family, to Jane certainly. She would never marry, not with her heart so branded by Darcy. She would have to shake this.

Perhaps she'd simply teach everyone's children. She'd be the governess she never had herself.

She smiled a wry smile that did not reach her eyes.

The door to the home opened, and Charlotte came

running, causing her to smile for real, with a happiness that started in her stomach. What a gift to have a best friend.

Perhaps she would have a good visit after all. If only she could avoid too many thoughts of Darcy. Surely she'd not see him again.

Chapter Twenty-Five

Darcy could feel no peace. No matter what position he found himself in his bed, sleep would not come. His thoughts were plagued with Elizabeth. Angry Elizabeth, happy Elizabeth, laughing Elizabeth, disdainful Elizabeth, and most terribly, hurt Elizabeth. She had been so tenderly aching, so much a shell of the vibrant person he had left. He could only blame himself for such a state.

It was a shock to see her, and she probably felt equally unsettled at the surprise. Perhaps she was more well off than she appeared. Perhaps he was only seeing the immediate shock, and she had her moments of strength. But no matter what, he could never forgive himself for being responsible for so much hurt in the woman he loved.

His heart shuddered. Woman he loved.

He'd admitted such strength of feeling before. But now,

it was accompanied by such a sense of responsibility. Duty or no, did he not have a duty to his heart? To the woman he loved? At least to see to her happiness, at least to ensure she was cared for as much or as well as Miss Anne?

He himself was certainly not well off. He was a bumbling emotional mess, trying to do his best to forget his heart to do his duty. And failing. Obviously failing.

And with Anne unavailable for the next few days, he had seen no reason, no reminder of how much she needed him, to grant motivation to stay the course. Instead, he now wanted nothing more than to find Elizabeth, to visit the Collinses' home, to never leave her side.

But she had said to leave her be, to let her forget.

How could he? The last thing he would ever want her to do would be to forget him.

But she must. If she would ever move on, to find her own happiness, she must forget him. He must orchestrate her happiness, ensure her well-being. He would never let her know, of course.

He threw the covers off and arose from bed. The prison of the darkness and discomfort of a bed that did not offer the solace of sleep were too much for him to bear a moment longer. He reached for a robe and tied it about himself. Perhaps he would find some distraction in the library. He could begin his plans to ensure the well-being of two women. One he must marry perhaps, and one he could not.

He gripped his hands into fists. The promise made to

his mother was harder than ever. If only he could speak with her once more. If he could hear her voice, counsel with her. If she had met Elizabeth, would she have seen what he did? Would she have approved of Darcy following his heart?

He could never know.

With a candle flickering in his grip, he made his way to the library. The house seemed empty. He decided he quite preferred not being surrounded by servants all the time. His own felt more like family. These felt as though they reported to his aunt, which of course they did. And he did not like that invasion of his privacy, nor the manipulation that happened as a result.

The library was lit in the back by a particularly bright moon. He made his way to the back window, where the silver light shone in, illuminating a small table and armchair. He knew the chair to be particularly comfortable, as he'd sat there many times, staring out at the grounds.

He wandered toward the family section of shelves. He would find some history of his family to read. Perhaps he'd be inspired by one of the past ancestors and their decisions on behalf of the estates. Had they ever struggled with marriage? How had their unions come to be? He'd never considered such a thing. His parents had married for love. The strength of feeling between them had always been a great comfort to him. But beyond them, in all those portraits on his walls at home, how had they chosen their wives? How had they managed their families?

He was well familiar with the books, the financials, the tenants, and the ventures that had brought about great wealth for their family and estate. He was equally aware and versed in the books at Rosings. Tonight, he wanted to connect with these great men from his past personally.

He held the candle up, looking at familiar tomes, ledgers, histories. He stopped on a thin, worn green cover. He pulled it out. He'd not noticed it before.

Inside were handwritten entries with a date at the top. It appeared to be a diary. He looked closer. The handwriting seemed familiar. His heart beat stronger. He turned back to the inside cover. The light flickered and he tilted the book to avoid a shadow on the name at the very top. His mother's name.

He swallowed back a lump in his throat. With fingers curled around the book, he cradled it until he sat down in the armchair. With the moon and candle lighting the words, he squinted to read his mother's words. "What do you have to tell me, Mother?"

The little journal began in what looked to be right before Darcy was born.

"My dearest little son, or at least I think you are a son. If you are my daughter, you are equally dear. I long to meet you. Not simply because you are making yourself known to me with your jabs and pushes inside, but because I am ready for you to make yourself known to the world. You will have much on your shoulders, much expected of you and many eyes on

you. Your aunt Catherine is also about to give birth to her child. It is our dearest hope that you will both be the closest of friends."

Darcy swallowed. They were intent on a relationship between the cousins from the very beginning.

"It is now high time you arrived, dear son. I feel you must be my son. It just seems like you could only be a son. Perhaps a mother knows. Perhaps not. I have plans for you. Maybe nights of reading stories to you, stories of the men who have gone before in our family, telling stories of your father's youth. You will be a joy to us both."

He skipped ahead. His mother wrote many entries of her great love for him. She was delighted with his smile, his health, his happiness. She said the nursemaid was most thrilled with his progress. He skipped more pages.

"Your cousin Anne has come to visit this summer, and I do admit to feeling some trepidation about her situation. My dear sister has changed so drastically since the birth of her daughter and the death of her husband. I never did think they were good together, but now I see that in many ways, he was not stifling her, but saving her and their daughter from herself. I'm afraid that left unchecked, she will be a detriment to herself and our dear sweet Anne. We must plan together, son, how to best lead Anne, how to help her make her way, and how to help her find a good situation when the time is right, so that she can be happy. I hope for her what I hope for you, which is a lovely marriage like your father and I have."

He was astounded at the news in this entry. At least in the beginning, it was never his mother's intention that he marry Anne. Instead, she hoped that perhaps he would help her find a good match.

He leaned back in his chair, breathing out very slowly as he pondered the implications of her words. Of course it was likely she had changed her mind in the next few years and begun to then hope for their marriage? Perhaps his aunt had used her manipulation on her to such an extent? Or perhaps she did truly wish for him to marry Anne.

He would keep reading, now knowing that his mother's initial wishes were not as his aunt described. They had not spent their moments since birth planning for them to marry. Initially, his mother was concerned enough about his aunt that she only wished to assist the young girl to find her way in life and to find happiness despite her mother.

He closed the book and tucked it away in an inner pocket of his robe. He had much to think about.

Chapter Twenty-Six

After two days of sticking to the gardens at the Collinses' home, assisting Charlotte in her daily tasks, and listening to Mr. Collins pontificate about any number of topics, Elizabeth needed to get out of the house. She assumed that there was very little chance she'd run into Mr. Darcy, and besides, she knew she was strong enough to send him away because she had done so already. With good powerful thoughts to buoy her up and a restlessness to rival any force in the world, Lizzy set out to walk as long and as far as her legs could carry her.

She bundled up, it being a colder morning, and set out down the lane. She'd been eyeing a particular grove of trees that were well spaced. It looked as though there might even be a river somewhere in there. She hurried down the lane, her feet not moving as quickly as she would like. There was so much to explore and not enough time to do it.

But she was determined to at least distance herself from her small environment of the last few days. She had thinking to do, and it wasn't happening in such close quarters.

The air was crisp. The sun was out. The colors were glorious and the sky was blue. The air had a smell to it. Sweet. And earthy. And a bit like rain on wet earth. The further she walked, the stronger the smell. She couldn't place it. But as she crested the hill, ordered groves spread out in front of her. "Fruit trees," she breathed. She not seen many in her life. They did not grow much in Longbourn. But here were rows and rows of something. She hurried to investigate. She neared the first tree and reached up to tug on a branch so that it was close enough to see. Apples.

"Oh, delicious." She breathed in the smells. Sweetness filled the air. The earth, the moisture, it was all there, all the smells that had been enticing her forward.

And a sound.

Horse hooves approaching.

She turned in place, searching for the source. A man atop a horse. Samson. She'd know that horse anywhere, and the rider.

He approached directly toward her, as though he knew already where to find her. She waited. What else could she do? There was nowhere to hide, though she wanted nothing more than to run.

He slowed a great distance from her, far enough that she

knew he was showing her great deference as opposed to their first meeting. She had to smile.

In response, his grin filled his face. "Have I learned something since our first meeting?"

"You have indeed," she called out. Perhaps they could have a congenial meeting of friends.

He leapt down from his horse and then let him roam freely. Samson immediately started to graze at the grass beneath their feet.

Darcy moved slowly, but his eyes were intent, as though he wanted to memorize every bit of her face before he stood any closer.

At last, he bowed and reached for her hand. With lips pressed to her bare skin, he lingered there, moving them over her knuckles, reminding her clearly of what it had been like to have those same lips explore hers.

Even though the sensation was dangerous, she could not have pulled her hand away if all the world depended on it. Desire climbed up her arm and into her chest, striking her core in shooting tingles that could not be ignored. She stepped closer and then rocked back and forth on her toes as she resisted the urge to throw herself into his arms. "Darcy." Her whispered plea filled the air around them.

His gaze lifted to hers and he straightened, but kept her hand in his. "I admit to calling at the house and heard the direction of your walk. Do you mind terribly the company?" His gaze was apologetic, but she knew he was determined.

"I do admit to feeling curious about what you would tell me before."

"There are new developments, of which I am not at liberty to express as of yet, but which give me hope." He began to walk, placing her hand in the crook of his arm. "But I had to see you simply to see you."

No clarity was offered in that brief explanation. She knew no more than she'd ever known about the mysterious Mr. Darcy. But at the moment, she was simply happy to be with him. Perhaps he would reveal more.

"How is Mrs. Collins?"

"She is well. They seem content. She's adjusted to her married life rather well, I'd say."

"And it is no doubt great to see your friend."

"Yes, of course. We have talked of all the things that must be discussed by two friends intent on solving all the ails in their friends' lives. Perhaps in the world itself." She smiled.

He chuckled. "I'd dare say the two of you could do a good amount to solve more problems than you realize. Heaven help us all."

She laughed. "Oh, you would only be so blessed to be in the circle of our awareness."

He paused in their walk and turned to her, showing his sincerity in his expression. "I am only too aware how blessed

I am to know you." He cleared his throat. "And what ails of mine would you solve?" His eyes twinkled with mischief.

"Oh, the very first one would be your inability to smile in large groups of people."

A laugh burst forth unexpectedly, so full of immediate pure enjoyment that she could only laugh along with him.

"See, more of that would be most welcome."

"But someone might see and know that I have a friendly side . . ." He grimaced with mock horror.

"Why would that be so bad?"

He seemed to consider her question with a moment of sincerity. "If they know it's possible, they will expect it of me every time, and I don't know if I can provide such on demand." He wiggled an eyebrow and she laughed in response.

He rested a hand on top of hers, still tucked in at his elbow. "But in truth, I don't always feel comfortable showing the very real parts of myself to strangers. I don't feel comfortable and I don't know exactly how to be so vulnerable with people I don't know." He glanced at her and looked away. "Perhaps that doesn't sound like the strong leader I should be . . ."

"On the contrary, I completely understand not wanting people aware of your close affairs. People don't always treat our most vulnerable and soft parts of our hearts with the gentleness they deserve."

"And . . ." He cleared his throat again. "Some women

get the wrong idea immediately."

She stiffened and tried to pull her hand away, but he held it tight. "And some women refuse to see the right idea no matter how often it is presented to them." He turned to stand in front of her. "Elizabeth. I don't know how I have survived these weeks without you." The pain in his face was almost too much.

"What are you doing?" Her lips quavered. "You can't say these things." He shouldn't even be walking with her if he couldn't resist toying with her. Unless he was at last willing to declare himself, to leave behind what held him. "Darcy. What holds you bound?" She was afraid to know at the same time that she longed to understand. At least with all the information, she could know how to move forward in her life. Perhaps if she, too, could support his reasons, then she could even make the sacrifice. She sighed. "I need to know."

"I have a cousin." He looked away. "She is dear to me and to my mother. And she is in the worst possible situation. When my mother passed, she made me promise to care for her, to ensure her well-being, and my aunt for years has declared that it was their most fervent wish that I marry my cousin. She acts as though we are engaged, reminds me weekly of my duty."

He ran a hand through his hair, mussing it in a way Elizabeth wasn't certain most people ever saw. And she'd inspired such a state of disarray often in the man. She watched him closely. What new developments had he realized?

"And do you like this cousin? Love her?" She held her breath.

"I do."

Her heart pounded slower in great thumps of dread.

"But not as one would wish to love his wife, if one wished for a marriage of love and not simply convenience."

She released her breath slowly. "And is that what you want? A marriage of love?" She searched his face, seeing nothing but the mask he always wore. Darcy was generally an enigma to most.

But he leaned closer so his eyes met hers. Their depths revealed so much more to him than anything else ever showed. She knew whatever he was about to say, he felt at his core. "I wish to love my wife most ardently, most completely, with everything this heart can muster. I wish it to be hers—my trust, my love, my children, my estate, my future, all hers." His eyes misted, and hers fully welled.

"That is the most beautiful thing I've ever heard." She tried to shake the emotion, but it gripped her and held her bound in his gaze. "Does your mother know?"

He looked down. "She passed. And her deathbed wish was for me to care for Anne." He turned away.

Elizabeth's hopes fell. "I'm sorry."

He seemed more distant every breath she took. He started walking again, this time without her hand on his arm. "And so, my quest is to determine just what my mother wished for me. And just what I want for myself." He shook his head. "And I feel bound to duty until I am certain that I am honoring her."

"And yourself."

"Pardon?" He still would not look at her.

"Your duty to yourself. Honoring yourself, your wishes. How can you be Darcy of Pemberley if you are not honoring who Darcy really is?"

"That sounds like a selfish excuse to do whatever I want. And believe me, my life has never been about me. I am the heir to Pemberley first. Darcy second." His tone warned her to let it go.

Elizabeth wished to say so much more, but held her tongue, as she was hardly an unbiased listener. She wanted more than anything for him to let go of whatever obligations he had and declare his love for her. In her most reckless moments, she dreamed of him doing exactly that. But those feelings were suppressed most of the time out of respect for her own emotional survival. This meeting in the woods was only complicating her own feelings and erasing whatever patience she'd tried to cultivate. She would never be rid of her desire for Darcy, at least not for many years to come, especially if he continued to appear in her life. "Perhaps it is time for me to return."

He stood taller. "Or at least for me to let you walk in peace." He bowed. "Thank you for your time." He turned on his heels, whistled for his horse, then leapt up on his back and rode away without another glance.

Chapter Twenty-Seven

Darcy had thought he'd figured it all out after reading his mother's journals, thought he would be able to declare himself to Elizabeth, but in the very moment he would have thrown everything at her feet, would have lowered to a knee, even, and asked to marry her, he realized he was still unsure. And he knew that he and Anne must have a conversation before he could say anything further to Elizabeth.

When he arrived back at the Rosings stables, he tossed the reins to the groomsman and went in search of Anne.

Elizabeth huffed and inwardly seethed as she pushed her way her forward on her walk. She was still miles from the Collinses' home. And she was tired. But she had much emotion to walk off and she knew it was better she not arrive through Charlotte's front door in such a state.

She was so torn between hating Darcy and loving him, between wanting to pound his chest in frustration and craving the softness of his arms and the warmth of his lips. She pressed hers together. That could never happen again. How could he open up such a torrent in her again? How could he fill her with hope and then close off again? This would all end as it had before, with Darcy doing his duty and she being left to herself.

She turned to cross the lane and walk through some of the Rosings Park estate. That would add interest for her return walk. Charlotte had assured her that the grounds would be open to her whenever she liked. Apparently, Lady Catherine De Bourgh was as involved in Charlotte's life and home as Mr. Collins had predicted. She even assisted in some adjustments to the home and shelves and closets to make it more useful. They were grateful recipients. Elizabeth might tire of such attentions, but the two of them seemed to need her and appreciate her input.

Elizabeth set out across a great green expanse of land. In the distance, the top of the estate building rose up on a hill. Spots dotted with trees decorated the otherwise rolling green. She was filled with a desire to run.

The woman she saw the day she arrived came to mind. Who was she? And what had happened when she, too, had started to run? Elizabeth looked in a full circle for anyone who would see the spectacle of her running across a field, and spotting no one, she picked up her skirts and took off at a full run across the grass.

At first, her chest complained, but after a moment of full breaths of air, she felt a burst of exhilaration, and the simple freedom of running where she liked, how she liked, filled her. With a great loud laugh, she tore across the lawn faster and faster, picking up speed, and raced with no destination in mind. She hardly saw her surroundings, just filled her lungs over and over with the sweet smells of the earth, the grass, and a hint of something floral. At last, when she thought her lungs would burst, she stopped, heaving for more air. She rested her hands on her thighs and took a moment to let her breath catch up.

When she raised her head again, she took in her surroundings. She stood at the edge of a thicker gathering of trees.

And she heard voices.

She turned to leave, wanting nothing more than to be alone.

But before she could make herself invisible, a young woman and two children came out into the clearing.

They all stopped as if frozen in place—Elizabeth, the woman, and her two children. And then Elizabeth laughed. “It seems as though none of us wish to be discovered.” She raised a hand. “Please pretend we never saw each other.” She turned from them, about to make her way in another direction. She had a long journey to return back to the Collinses' at this point.

"Wait."

Elizabeth almost groaned.

"You are Mrs. Collins's friend, are you not?"

She turned back. Now she must make the appropriate motions to maintain the respect of her friend in the area. "I am indeed. She is the best of friends. I'm here visiting with her family."

"I'm so pleased to meet you. I do believe my mother has invited you all to dinner this evening."

"Has she! Your mother . . . Lady Catherine?"

She nodded. "I am her daughter, Lady Anne De Bourgh."

Elizabeth dipped in a curtsey. "And I'm Miss Elizabeth. I'm so happy to meet you and terribly sorry I have disturbed what seems to be a lovely outing." She looked on with curiosity at the children.

"Oh, forgive me. These are some of the tenant farmer's children and my dear friends." She looked down at the young girl. "This is Scarlet and Teddy. They are as dear as anyone you would ever meet and have offered to keep me company on my walk."

They looked up with such adoring faces that Elizabeth suspected they were dear indeed. She decided to love this woman for her goodness to the tenants. She was definitely of the character of someone Elizabeth would value.

"We would welcome the addition if you'd like to continue your walk with us." Lady Anne frowned. "Have you come all this way on foot?"

"I have indeed. I found myself in much need of the outdoors, and it has been the best sort of diversion, mostly."

"We shall call for the carriage for your return, shall we not? Spare you the walk? I do believe you might wish the time to prepare for dinner. My mother unfortunately demands we all eat in formal attire."

Elizabeth nodded, and then stepped to her side to join their walk. "Were you out running the other day?"

Lady Anne's face colored. "You saw that?"

"I'm sorry. I only ask because it was you who inspired me to run just now." She giggled. "It was delicious."

"Isn't it wonderful when you need a good run to just throw caution away and let your feet run as far and as fast as they can?"

"The freedom." Elizabeth smiled and then laughed. "I see you understand."

"I dearly love to run. As someone who suffers from the inability to run or exert myself often, I cherish moments when I am able."

Her phrasing was a bit odd, but Elizabeth was grateful not to be plagued with any health ailments. As she fell in step with Lady Anne, the children ran about together, playing a newfound game.

"I'm sorry to scare off your friends."

Though she looked after them wistfully, she shook her head. "They need to run about. I can't keep up."

"Do you suffer from fatigue?"

She looked into Elizabeth's face with a particular intensity. "I do. But it is not a true health problem. I suffer from fatigue of being coddled and protected and controlled." She pressed a hand to her heart. "I am so sorry. I should not complain. Who is evil enough to resist the efforts of a woman who only wishes to love and care for me?"

"Your mother?"

She nodded. "I am afraid if I let her keep me locked up as she has, I shall never recover. Consumption once as a girl, and perhaps a predilection to catch it again, but since then, no expense or treatment has been spared to keep me from dying." She shook her head. "I do believe the loss of my father and her sister have changed my mother into a person I never knew as a young girl."

Lady Anne breathed in slowly. "She used to ride sidesaddle across the back property when no one was looking. She was daring, bold—fun, even." She kicked a bit of a root with her foot. "But no longer. Now she spends her waking moments clinging to my health and protecting me from so many things, I think I'm failing because of it."

Elizabeth didn't respond, just walked at her side. In truth, Lady Anne probably almost forgot she'd spoken at all. Or at least, to a stranger.

* * *

Darcy entered unannounced into his aunt's private sitting room, with two servants in tow. "Where is Anne?"

She lifted surprised eyes from her needlepoint. "In her rooms. If you recall, she's using the next couple days to recover from all the exertion of your visit." She smiled. "It is rather endearing to see you so enamored, though, Darcy. I do hope you can learn to love your cousin in a way that leads to a happy life together. Your mother and I both wished it."

He could hardly stand the repetition. It had been repeated so oft, he could not envision his aunt's face without the accompanying petition to remember his mother's fondest wish.

"Was it her fondest wish, Aunt? Or yours?"

"Pardon? What do you mean, Darcy? Of course it was hers and mine. You remember, she told you herself."

"We don't have the time to talk about that right now. Anne is not in her rooms. No one knows where she is."

"That's ridiculous. Of course she's in her rooms." She reached for a hand-held bell and rang it.

Two maids stepped into the room and bobbed their curtsies. "Is Miss Anne in her rooms?"

"Yes, my lady. She is there taking her morning sleep. We have servants on the clock monitoring and watching her as you asked." They did not meet her eyes, of course, but even with the normal servant deference hiding almost all emotion, Darcy could tell something was hidden. Something wasn't exactly as they were sharing.

But Lady Catherine seemed satisfied. Darcy decided not to keep pressing, even though he knew she was not there. He'd visited just moments before, but if the servants were denying her absence, then perhaps she had them covering for her. Either way, he would investigate a bit further before asking for a search.

He was left alone again in the room with his aunt. They each said nothing for a matter of moments, until at last, Darcy broke the silence. "I am not enamored with my cousin."

Lady Catherine paused in her needlepoint but did not glance up at him. "Perhaps you cannot see it, but the love you have for her is obvious to everyone else." She smiled softly to herself.

"I do love her, that is true."

She looked up, triumphant.

But he shook his head. "But not in the way a husband should love his wife."

She tsked her tongue and shook her head. "You young people have such grand and overly fantastical notions about marriage." She flicked her fingers and then returned to her needlepoint. "The truth is, love confuses things. Love makes us do crazy things, things that make us unhappy, things that lead us down illogical paths, directions that do not promise the greatest success."

"But love makes sure that whatever path we take, we make it last. We weather the storms, the illogical, the nonsensical, and we do it triumphantly with great joy. Because we love the person at our side."

Her face lined with pain for the briefest of moments before she sighed and sat back in her chair in a rare form of slouched posture. "What you don't yet know, Darcy, is that even the truest form of love will one day fade, falter, and betray." She closed her eyes as if trying to stave off difficult memories. "Your best chance of happiness is to not place yourself in such a vulnerable position as love to begin with. Go into things with a level head and a strong friendship, which you and Anne have in great abundance. You both are smart and have the needs of the family foremost in your minds. You will ensure the permanence of both our estates. It is the best decision by far that either of you could make."

She sat upright again. "What do you know of the simpletons you meet in London? Nothing of note. You know they are poised and speak of the weather with great wit. But can they weather any storm? Do they truly care about Pemberley? Your servants? Your tenants?" She shook her head. "You won't know until it is too late. Far better to marry familiarity. You two get along so well. Your mother would be most pleased that the smallest desire of our hearts has grown to something that promises to be successful indeed."

"Just exactly what did my mother say to you about my marrying?"

She did not meet his eyes as she took up her needlepoint again. But he knew what she would say before she said it. She'd repeated the same words over and over since he was a young lad. And now, he didn't believe a word of them, not after reading his mother's journal.

He bowed and excused himself. It was time to do some further reading of his mother's last entries, right after he found just where Anne had absconded.

Chapter Twenty-Eight

Anne was a delightful conversationalist. She spoke of everything and anything, and all of it interesting. But mostly she wished to know of life at Longbourn. What was it like with so many sisters, and most especially how was it to be so involved with the local gentry. "I do not have many friends, you see. I see almost no one, rarely socialize, and have very litte opportunity. I know how to dance because of an instructor, but have never been asked formally to dance."

Her expression took on a hint of the secretive and Elizabeth was immediately intrigued. "But you have danced, haven't you?" She smiled, inviting a confidence.

Anne reached for her hands and squeezed. "I have, and it was so delicious. No one can know, of course, but we had such a time of it, he whistling a tune and I dancing at his side for every country reel that we knew."

Elizabeth's mouth dropped. "Lady Anne, you have a secret admirer, don't you?"

Her eyes gleamed with love. And Elizabeth was astounded at the strength in them. She could only hope to understand love in the way that Anne's eyes shone.

"I do. Though it's not secret to me. We wish most desperately to be together."

"What is holding you back?"

She looked away and shrugged.

"Your mother?"

"Yes. It is quite complicated. But I am promised elsewhere, and she just doesn't think of this man as worthy of me."

"But are you not able to marry whom you choose? So long as they are gentry, of course."

She shifted uncomfortably.

"Unless he is not?"

"That's part of what makes the explanation complicated. He is indeed respectable. He was meant to have the clergy position here in the home that abuts Rosings."

"Which was given to Mr. Collins?"

She nodded. "And I do hope you know I mean your cousin no ill will."

"Do not trouble yourself. He is cousin in name only. I barely know him."

"Mother found out about our attachment, this man and me, and strove to do everything in her power to make an alignment between us impossible. She denied him the rectorate, refused her financial sponsorship for another position, nor her recommendation, and forced his hand in the caring for one specific tenant family here on the estate."

"How so?"

"They are his relations. He has been blessed enough to rise above, a gift from Lord De Bourgh, a reward for his good and loyal service. He was trained in the clergy and was promised a position."

Elizabeth nodded. "And Lady Catherine is too terrible to deny him. I can't account for it."

"It is her wish that I align myself with a cousin instead. In truth, it would be a finer match, an opportunity to preserve the estate against future years of scarcity. But I admit, I care nothing about that or even my title. I would live as a tenant farmer if I could but stay with Rolf." She sighed. "But Mother threatened me. She discovered my many attempts to see him and told me that if I did not carry on in my marriage to D—the other one, that she would send the tenant family away, my Rolf along with them."

"Forgive me, but how can a mother behave so?"

"She thinks she is seeing things more clearly and that she is truly blessing my life."

Lizzy nodded, remembering an attempt by her mother to force her into marrying Mr. Collins. "Heaven help us to never behave as our mothers."

"Amen."

A servant came riding toward them in a cart. As soon as he was near enough, he dipped his head from his position in the cart. “Forgive me. We must make haste. There are inquiries as to your whereabouts.”

“Oh dear. My outings end too soon. Could I get you to take Miss Elizabeth back to the Collinses’ home? I shall accompany the children. I believe I can use the cart we left at the farm.”

“Very good, my lady.”

While being helped up into the cart, Elizabeth turned to her new friend. “I’m so pleased we have met. I shall do all in my power to aid in your situation.”

Anne’s eyes turned soft with hints of sorrow. “Thank you. But I have little hope. My mother is not like others you may have met. Very few dare to cross her.”

Chapter Twenty-Nine

Darcy found no further clues as to where Anne had gone. Her servants were of the most loyal kind, and for that he was grateful. Perhaps she would be able to fend for herself. She was much stronger than she seemed. And the fact that she had agreed so readily to be in bed and then had left straightaway and not with him showed that she had agendas of her own and things she would like to be doing. The woman was not as controlled and manipulated as he thought, to a point.

He returned to his rooms, where his valet informed him of guests coming for dinner and a formal dress requirement. Curse his aunt and her old-fashioned eating requirements. Very few insisted on formal attire for dinner. He could see a cravat, naturally, but to wear a ball jacket and his nicest boots and all the things required for him to present himself before royalty? The problem being, naturally, that royalty were nowhere near Rosings. His aunt had noble blood, as did he. But they certainly did not need to stand on ceremony for one another.

He grumbled through most of his servant's ministrations and was about to descend in the foulest of all moods when Anne peeked her head in the doorway. She was dressed in a beautiful gown and looked healthier and happier than he had ever seen her.

He hurried to the doorway. "Anne. You look well." He bowed over her hand and searched her face, but she revealed nothing.

"I am well. I am quite well. I do believe the rest has done wonders for me. I shall not suffer from the exertions of having you here, never fear, cousin." She stepped aside to allow him to exit his room.

He did so and offered his arm. "I know you were not in your rooms."

She smiled. "So the servants told me."

"Are you going to share what you were doing that has you in the best of moods?"

"Not likely."

He nodded. "And will you be stuck to your rooms tomorrow as well?"

"That is likely, I'm afraid."

He laughed. "Then I can only be pleased on your behalf. I hope whoever the man is, that he realizes how lucky he is."

She choked on her next words, whatever they might have been. "Pardon me?" With a hand at her heart, she turned wide eyes and an open mouth on him.

"Have I presumed in error?" His turn for wide eyes gave him a great amount of enjoyment. His pretended innocence made her smile.

"You are quite correct, though you are the only one to be so correct in this entire household. Everyone else thinks I am about the service to our dear tenants." She shook her head. "Which is not entirely untrue, naturally."

"Naturally." He waited, watching her with great curiosity and a growing sense of euphoria.

"But you mustn't say a word and you must know that this . . . these meetings, they can come to nothing. I must not be able to pursue any sort of relationship past this spring. It was with the intent to say farewell that I initiated another meeting, actually."

The weight in his stomach returned. "And why? If you are so happy, why can it not be?"

"You of all people should know."

"Should I?"

"Mother does not approve. I'm to marry you. To fulfill our—our duty. Not to mention that he is currently technically a tenant farmer himself." She stared only at her feet with those last words, and he wasn't certain how to respond.

After an uncomfortable set of three breaths, he rested a hand on her shoulder. "And do you love him?"

She sniffed and wiped her eyes. "I do. And his children."

Alarm ricocheted through his chest. "Children?"

She nodded and covered her face with her hands. "It is so perfect, as we aren't certain I shall ever have some of my own. Don't you see how it's perfect? We love each other. A ready family." She clutched at his jacket lapel. "I don't see why I cannot have what is perfect."

"Why did you say technically a tenant farmer? How could one technically be a tenant farmer? What other kinds of tenant farmers are there?" He smiled to himself.

"Well, that's the crux of the problem right there, cousin, because he was meant to be a clergy member, with the rectory that Mr. Collins now inhabits."

Darcy could make no sense of her words. But Lady Catherine stepped out into the hall. "What are you two about? We have guests. We must be about our dinner." She paused. "Anne. It is good to see you up and about. I must say, the rest has done your coloring a world of good. Don't you agree, Darcy?"

"I do indeed. It's amazing what a good rest can do to a person."

Anne's mouth twitched, but the look of warning she sent in his direction had him choking on a laugh straightaway. He held out his arm. "Come now. We must entertain the subservient subjects in your mother's realm."

"Realm, you say. You are nonsensical, Fitzwilliam. But we shall dine indeed. I've invited the Collinses. I do so appreciate his excellent service in that rectory. Is he not the most wonderful man to fill the position, Anne?"

She stiffened with her hand on his arm. And Darcy could not understand why a mother would behave so to her daughter. Why had she given the rectory to another? Why would she then bring it up again to her daughter? He could not understand.

They made their way down the stairs to prepare to greet their guests. Darcy planned to have a devil of a time trying to pretend happiness in supporting his aunt or interest in talking with strangers, until he heard one particular laugh.

Anne squeezed his arm. "Oh, I'm so pleased. It's Miss Elizabeth! I'd know her laugh anywhere."

"You know Miss Elizabeth?"

"Of course, she's come to stay with the Collinses . . . Wait, how do you know Miss Elizabeth?"

They turned the corner in full view of the dinner guests.

Mr. and Mrs. Collins and Miss Elizabeth turned to face them.

"Mr. Darcy!" A very shocked-looking Elizabeth turned white as a sheet.

Chapter Thirty

Lady Catherine swept into the room. "Miss Elizabeth, are you acquainted with my nephew?"

Elizabeth removed the hand from her mouth and attempted a curtsy and some semblance of good manners in the face of the total upheaval wreaking havoc in her stomach. How was Mr. Darcy here?

He stood tall, as handsome as ever, and even though he was much better than she at hiding his emotions, the look of pleasure in his face upon seeing her warmed her to the very tips of her toes. She would do anything to hold fast to that pleasure, to always be the cause of his happiness. She would be his love if he would let her. And she was hopeless for any kind of escape from him. She thought that she might possibly one day be free of him, but seeing him again, she knew that she was lost forever. There would simply always be a part of her that longed for Mr. Darcy. Let that be a lesson to all young people thinking there was such a thing as a harmless flirtation. Harmless indeed. She was changed forever. Doomed to eternal misery.

But she could not continue with these thoughts, not with him right in the room, not under the scrutiny of Lady Catherine. She placed a hand at her stomach. Somehow she must calm the storm that abided there and behave as a normal person in front of everyone.

She had been asked a question. What was it now? Lady Catherine waited expectantly.

"Oh, erm. Yes, I am acquainted with him. He accompanied his friend Mr. Bingley to Netherfield, where we were introduced."

"Ah yes, naturally. And how is Longbourn? I know Mr. Collins is particularly fond of your estate."

Elizabeth gritted her teeth. Normally such a comment could be hidden away beneath a bit of wit, but not today. She was barely able to form a coherent thought.

Luckily, Charlotte assisted her. "She has been filling us in on all the details. It is a fine estate, one which I visited quite often as a child and into maidenhood."

Lady Catherine looked as though she would ask more, but Lady Anne placed her hand on Darcy's arm. "I do believe it might be time to enter for dinner?"

"Yes, you are correct." Lady Catherine placed her hand on Darcy's other arm and the three entered first. Mr. Collins followed with Charlotte on his arm. He did not offer an arm to Elizabeth, which she found most vexing only as a matter of decorum. He would be considered quite rude in most circles. But Sir Lucas, who should have entered before Mr. Collins, arguably, offered his other arm, and Elizabeth entered the room with her dear friends the Lucases.

Now she must understand how Mr. Darcy was acquainted with Lady Anne and her mother. She had her suspicions. And they were growing stronger by the second as Lady Catherine's proprietary air over Darcy and Anne became more apparent. She sniffed in approval as Darcy helped Anne to her chair.

But then he hurried to Elizabeth's side and did the same for her. He then sat at her side, leaving Anne and Lady Catherine to be entertained by the Collinses.

Elizabeth hid her smile at the narrowed eyes of Lady Catherine. She spoke quietly to Darcy. "I do believe you have vexed our hostess."

Darcy's eyes darted to Lady Catherine's and then away, but he did not comment. After signaling that the servant should fill their cups, he leaned close and murmured, "I would not miss an opportunity to sit at your side no matter whom I vex."

She bit her cheek to keep from forming her own triumphant expression. "I'm making all kinds of assumptions here."

"As am I. How do you know my cousin?"

"Your . . . cousin?" She swallowed. "And betrothed?" It was her turn for narrowed eyes.

"Not at all. Is that what she told you?" The earnestness in his expression told Elizabeth he might be as unaware as Lady Anne as to the nature of their relationship. Truth be told, Elizabeth herself wasn't told as much. She was gathering all information by bits and pieces of her observation and could be incorrect at any turn.

"Our relationship is complicated. As I have tried to express my situation being the same," he said.

"But you said there are new developments?"

"What are you two whispering about?" Lady Catherine called down the table to them. "I will not have side conversations. I must know what is so interesting."

Elizabeth indicated that Darcy could be the one to handle his aunt. She let that idea settle more. Lady Catherine De Bourgh was his aunt. She could hardly believe fate or whatever it was with a sense of humor had arranged their meeting all together at Rosings. She, Charlotte, Mr. Collins, Darcy . . . It was too much and yet most perfectly perfect if the author of their lives had a wit about her.

But Anne did not love Darcy. She was in love with someone named Rolf. Did Darcy know such a thing? Her eyes met Anne's. And with the slightest shake of her head, Elizabeth knew her answer to that. What a complicated, perfectly orchestrated, messy plan. If all worked out in some sliver of a chance, perhaps the lot of them could be inexpressibly happy. Everyone except Lady Catherine, and she was the one not to be trifled with, everyone kept saying. But she had not yet met Elizabeth, who was also one not to be trifled with.

Darcy shifted beside her and found her hand under the table. "You look inordinately pleased. Should I be concerned?"

"If you don't know the cause, you should always be concerned." She laughed to herself. "I'm not certain it's yet warranted, but I'm imagining happiness for us all."

Hope lit like a fire in the back of Darcy's eyes. It was as if heaven itself had come to call, and she was stunned. Her mouth went dry, a thirst not even huge gulps of her water could quench. Darcy's taciturn distance was alluring, but his hopeful joy was irresistible, and she gave up trying to part with him.

No one should have to sacrifice that kind of joy for another. Joy would be available to all if they but lived after the manner of their own happiness. She had to believe such a thing were true. She had to believe in a providence like that, one who wished good for all, one who would help everyone make the best of their lives, no matter the circumstances. And she decided to make the best of hers.

She squeezed Darcy's hand in return, a small smile lingering on her face.

"I'm not certain what you have working itself through that mind of yours, but I long to hear it." He lifted a cup toward Lady Catherine. "Thank you, Aunt, for a delightful dinner, the fruits of which will last through the ages."

She beamed a glance at her daughter, but Anne looked from Darcy to Elizabeth with a slightly unsettled expression. Still, she raised her cup and the others fell suit. "To Lady Catherine."

* * *

After dinner, Anne moved to claim Darcy's arm. "I do believe we can forgo the separation where the men go to their cigars and port and the ladies to their gossip? Perhaps whist?" She indicated they walk together out the side door.

Darcy nodded. "Certainly." But he paused and offered his other arm to Elizabeth. "If I may?"

She nodded as well. "Certainly."

Mr. Collins rushed to offer his arm to Lady Catherine, even before doing so to his wife. The esteemed lady said little, but with raised eyebrows, allowed herself to be escorted by the Collinses from the room and into her drawing room.

Tables had been prepared and cards for whist placed. A small chess set sat in the corner, a little nook further from the others.

"Come, Miss Elizabeth." Lady Catherine's voice took on a demanding tone. "I must play you in a game of chess."

Both Elizabeth and Anne looked to Darcy with

concerned expressions, Anne's more alarmed and Elizabeth's more on fire. This was going to be an interesting evening.

He sat at a table with Anne and the Collinses. He remembered thinking Charlotte to be a sensible sort of woman. And she was quite adept at whist. She and Mr. Collins beat he and Anne soundly the first round. But it was because his and Anne's attention were both riveted to the pair playing chess. They did not have a view of Lady Catherine's expressions, but Elizabeth's were in plain sight and she hid very little.

Her eyebrows rose high on her brow for much of the conversation. At times, she shook her head slightly, and more often, adamantly. Anne and Darcy exchanged helpless expressions. Elizabeth seemed able to fend for herself, at least thus far in the conversation. She also appeared to be winning.

Darcy smiled to himself. She would win. And she just might be the woman to stand up to his aunt as well. He sat higher in his seat, pride in Elizabeth showing.

Anne's small smile grew. But her eyes were filled with concern.

Darcy tried to reassure her with his expression, but truth be told, she would need to be bold and daring on her own behalf too. Happiness was a gift, a precious opportunity one must seize when presented with its possibility. As he watched Miss Elizabeth say something with great animation to his aunt, he realized his happiness sat right in that corner.

He was about to stand and go to her when she herself stood. Her voice carried as she said, "And now you have insulted me in every possible way. I would ask you to hold your tongue or I must leave this instant."

"I will not have the shades of Pemberley be thus soiled by the likes of you."

Anne gasped and Darcy rushed to Elizabeth's side, but she waved him away and marched past, muttering, "Insufferable."

"Miss Elizabeth!" Lady Catherine called after her. "You will not turn your back on me. You will answer me this instant."

But her demands went unanswered and ignored as Elizabeth marched from the room and, Darcy presumed, out the front door.

He laughed to himself. But he daren't go after her, not with Anne trembling beside him, eyes on her mother, not with the rest of the evening to salvage. He would see Elizabeth tomorrow, properly, with a courtship in mind.

Chapter Thirty-One

Elizabeth refused to stay in the area one more moment. She would not be thus insulted, not be so mistreated in front of her friends, in front of Mr. Darcy, even, and then be forced to defend herself.

But she would not leave on account of offense. That would not be sensible. She would leave because of one sentence, one horribly true sentence. And because of its truth, she must not return, she must not entertain thoughts of Mr. Darcy or any sort of relationship there.

"He knows his duty lies with Anne. Do you think he would ever be truly happy knowing he'd defied his mother and left Anne to fend for herself, to live with tenant farmers?"

And with that, her anger heightened, but her reason broke through and she knew she would never be happy with a Darcy who was plagued with remorse for defying his mother and his duty.

She threw her clothes in a trunk, packed her bonnets, her boots, her letter-writing materials. She screwed the cap on the ink as tightly as she could. Then she used Charlotte's writing desk to leave her a note. She tried to be as lavish as possible in her praise and gratitude. Her friend would understand when the others likely would not.

And then she waited for the hired hack the servants had called for her. Bless the servants. Did anyone ever pause to think of the terrible efforts they all made on a family's behalf? Their young lad, Joshua, ran the distance to the square to inquire about a hack. She wished she had a coin to give the lad upon his return. She had very little, and she needed to make it all the way to London to her aunt and uncle. Long ago, they'd offered to take her on a lake country trip which was sounding more and more the thing.

Only when her trunk was loaded atop the carriage, and she seated tightly packed on a row with two others, did she allow herself the luxury of tears.

Her heart clenched and tightened in her chest in such a painful way, she was forced to gasp for air.

The woman just to her left patted her hand. "Sometimes a good cry does wonders for the complexion."

Lizzy didn't know what to make of that statement. She herself looked terrible after crying. But there was nothing for it. She hurt so terribly that she could do nothing but cry. How did one fall so completely in love and then survive after? For she didn't not know in that moment how she would do anything besides hurt.

Lady Catherine's words had been so particularly aimed at hurting her. She could not believe such was possible from a woman of good breeding. Apparently titles and education did nothing for goodwill and kindness.

"Did you plan to become engaged to my nephew?"

She'd been aghast at such a personal and poorly timed question.

"My plans are not your concern. And such a decision would be between two people, would it not?"

"But are you exerting your wiles on him, manipulating him into doing what is against his very nature, tempting him into performing against his will, his desires, and his duty?"

She could do nothing but deny one terrible accusation after another.

"And do you not admit to loathing my Anne?"

She'd gasped at that. *"How can you say such a thing? Of course I do not loathe her. I actually quite like her."*

"How can you say such a thing? How can you not love my Anne, she who suffers when you do not?"

She had nothing to respond with besides the truth, which was being doubted and questioned with every breath. But the longer she listened, the more clarity there was in her mind of her situation. She could have nothing more to do with Mr. Darcy. And even though that was likely the purpose to Lady Catherine's diatribe, it had been quite successful.

She didn't deserve such a man, not really, not by birth or station or wealth. She herself was uneducated besides what she'd attempted to teach herself. She knew nothing of managing a grand estate. And her mother had taught her nothing of proper decorum. She had no title or even name to recommend herself. Her uncle was in trade. She sat as far below Mr. Darcy as anyone. Her father was a gentleman, yes, but that was as far as she could boast.

She closed her eyes, trying to pretend she sat alone, in her woods behind their house at Longbourn. Perhaps she'd stay with her aunt and uncle until Jane's wedding. There was a happy thought to grab hold of. With any luck, that relationship was going well and bans would be posted soon.

Even though she'd given her aunt and uncle no notice, they welcomed her in with great happiness two days later as she arrived much beaten down. They called for a bath and had her tucked into a warm bed as soon as possible.

When she awoke on the morrow, her clothes were washed and packed, and they were talking of leaving for the lake country that afternoon.

She took tea with her aunt in their cozy morning room. "I'm sorry, Aunt, for the sudden change of plans."

"I can only be pleased." She eyed Elizabeth with great compassion. "And I shan't pry into your reasons. But you do know you are most welcome to burden me with any details you like. Sometimes talking through these things helps a great deal."

"I would like that when I'm ready."

Her uncle entered with several letters in hand. "I've a delightful proposition if you're both willing. What say you to a slight detour on our journey and a stop in Derbyshire?"

Her aunt clapped her hands. "Oh, you know I would love that above most things!"

Elizabeth smiled. At least Darcy would not be at Pemberley. Though it pained her to be so close to his ancestral home, she could not deny a certain curiosity. "I'd like that as well. You are too good to have me."

"We are most pleased you could come." Her aunt took hold of her hand. "You are like the daughter we could never have."

"Thank you. Perhaps I could stay longer, even after our trip?"

"Why, of course, if your mother can spare you."

Lizzy nodded. "She is most able to spare me." With a laugh, she added, "I hear often of how challenging it is for her to marry off all five of us. Perhaps with one less bearing down on her daily . . ." She grinned. "At any rate, I shall enjoy the respite."

"Then you shall stay as long as you like."

The love from her aunt and uncle filled her and healed the smallest portion of her heart. Though she doubted she'd ever shed the sense of loneliness that yearned for Darcy, she knew she could perhaps lessen the pain.

Her aunt stood. “We must rest up today, then, especially you after such a long journey. After tea, we will be off again. I do feel that your uncle’s equipage will be far more comfortable than the hired carriages you took.”

Elizabeth stood as well. “I shall be happy no matter what the journey brings. And I do think I am in need of more rest. I shall take to my bed until it is time to depart, if you don’t mind.”

Chapter Thirty-Two

Once the Collinses left for the evening, Darcy and Anne approached Lady Catherine.

"Mother, what did you say to Miss Elizabeth?"

Lady Catherine's eyes narrowed. "I simply said what needed to be said. We will not be plagued further by her, I assure you."

"I wouldn't be too certain. She's not to be trifled with or controlled." Darcy spoke with pride in her strength.

"Oh no? The servants tell me she has already left—a hired hack, of all things."

Darcy stood in alarm. "What? When?"

"Oh come, nephew. She has you in her trappings. Sit for a moment and allow some sense to return to your masculine sensibilities."

"Of all the ridiculous notions. You speak as if I do not have my full faculties."

He looked to Anne for some support, but she could only return his gaze with question in her eyes.

"You as well? You doubt me?"

Lady Catherine waved her fingers and answered for Anne. "We do not doubt you. We are certain of your sense of duty. We know you will do what is required of you. I just paved the path to a less painful resolution."

"But sending her on her way? Have you no care for the lady?"

"Not in the way I care for you or Anne, no." She sat tall, certain of herself.

"If you cared for me at all, you would see that my heart is engaged elsewhere." He turned to Anne to attempt to soften the blow. But she seemed unsurprised. And unfazed.

"And what does that matter? Your heart? Engaged elsewhere? As is mine."

Lady Catherine gasped and placed a hand at her chest.

Darcy's eyes narrowed. "Explain yourself."

"I love you, cousin. You are family to me. And I see our futures laid out perfectly together. I choose you and that and a duty to our great families and estates. But I love another. And I have come to accept that as a love which will never be mine to nurture further." Her mouth quivered for one brief moment, but then she pressed her lips together and turned open, honest eyes to Darcy. "I am ready to accept our future together."

Lady Catherine looked as though she might faint from holding her breath. He stood and took Anne's hand. "Might we have a word, alone?"

She nodded.

Lady Catherine's expression turned victorious. "The Blue Room has a lovely mantle in front of which I received my proposal."

He shook his head. "We shall go to Anne's personal sitting room, if you don't mind."

"Oh certainly, I'll send a servant to stand just outside the opened door."

He nodded and then placed Anne's hand on his arm. As soon as they were out of earshot, she murmured, "I was going to tell you."

"Before or after we were married?"

"Before, at your proposal. I was going to explain the whole situation so you could choose."

"And now? That charade in front of your mother?"

"It was not a charade."

He turned to her.

Her eyes were certain, her face calm. "Let us finish this conversation where others will not hear."

As soon as they entered her room, he closed the door. "Now please, explain yourself."

"I do love another. He was to have the rectory currently

held by Mr. Collins. I loved him dearly and my mother intervened. His family come from tenant farmers, some, and from an educated mother, whose father sent him to learn the ways of the church."

"So your mother disapproves."

"Naturally, on the grounds of hope for a connection to Pemberley, but also his questionable and tainted family."

"Tainted."

"I use her words, not mine. He is the most lovely man—his goodness shines from within—and I love his children like my own. I have indeed hoped them to be mine in my dreams every night."

"How does he have children?"

"His wife died, years ago. We became friends shortly after her death, when I paid a visit to console the children. For years we have been close. He is like family, and I love him with a passion that cannot be quenched." Her face flushed and her eyes shone with evidence of that love.

"What a beautiful blessing in your life." Darcy placed a hand at the side of her face. "One I think you should pursue and enjoy for the rest of your days."

"But Darcy, he is now but a tenant farmer, that is all. Mother would never allow it. She would turn the family out. We would have nothing. She has threatened to do as much if I do not do exactly as she requires. She will send them to a workhouse, all of them."

Light cleared Darcy's mind. "So this is what she holds over you, this is why you bow to her every wish."

She nodded. "I do not have to be his wife. It is enough to know he is cared for, that his children have a place here."

"And if you marry me?"

"She will arrange for him to have a rectory elsewhere." She sighed. "But of course, that's not the only reason I would marry you. I do care for you, Fitzwilliam. We get on well together."

"Certainly. We would most definitely have an easy match of things, if we weren't desperately in love with other people. What kind of happiness do you think we would have, both pining for another?"

"An understanding, empathetic one?"

"And I'm to have no heir?"

"We do not know my capacity in that regard as of yet. And there are other ways . . ."

He shook his head, abhorrence and alarm growing. "You do not expect me to—"

"Not if you are opposed, but these things can be arranged." She seemed unfazed by the possibility that Darcy would share a bed elsewhere.

He shook his head. "And do you suppose that you would then have relations, that you would see your man of the cloth on the side?"

She shook her head. "I would never. You know as well as

I do that men tend more toward these activities than women, at least that is what I am told."

"I would not give much credence to anything your mother says." He dug his fingers into his palms. "What I would do to put that lady in a dowager house far from all of us." He pinched the bridge of his nose. "Forgive me, Mother."

"There's something you must know," Anne said.

"What's that?"

"Your mother did not wish for us to marry necessarily. She only wished for you to care for me, to assist me against the wiles of my own mother."

His heart skipped one whole beat while he digested further proof of what he had suspected. "How can you know such a thing?"

"I read her journals." She held up a hand when he would interrupt. "Including the pages Mother removed and burned."

"She . . . burned them?"

"Are you really that surprised?

He considered her question. "I am not actually surprised at all. But sick to my stomach? Yes. Anne, I refuse for this to be our life."

She clutched at his arm. "What are you saying? You cannot deny me. Rolf and his whole family will go to the poorhouse."

Darcy shook his head. "They will not."

Her eyes flickered with hope and then faded to gray. She turned away. "You underestimate my mother."

"No. She underestimates me. Do not fret. I will make this right. And even if Elizabeth will never have another word to say to me, which I would not blame her, you shall have your happiness."

He headed for the door. "Pack your bags. You will leave with me to Pemberley this evening."

He opened the door to Lady Catherine standing just outside. "How dare you compromise my daughter in a room with just the two of you."

"Oh stop, Aunt. You can have nothing of which to accuse. We will not hear of it. No servant will spread the lies and no one else knows."

Lady Catherine's mouth dropped. "How dare you—"

"You can have nothing further to say. I am relieving Anne from your care. She is leaving this night with me and will be staying with her cousin Georgiana at Pemberley for the foreseeable future."

Her nostrils flared and her face went white as a sheet. "Take great care, Anne, for you know what hangs in the balance here."

"Rolf and his family?" Darcy shook his head. "I have a rectory position for him in Derbyshire, Aunt. You have lost our respect. You have sacrificed the happiness and well-being of your only daughter. You have attempted to force and manipulate your plans for us all. I will have no further upsets in my life and plans. I will not have you forcing such on us. We will move forward with the best hopes of our own personal happiness and that of our lineage in mind. You could have had Anne living across the street, all your days." He shook his head. Then he waved to the servants behind Lady Catherine. "Aid Miss Anne in the packing of her things. We leave in one hour."

Lady Catherine gasped. "You will not. I will not allow you to take my daughter from me."

"I can and I will. You, of course, are welcome to come. But you will be staying in the dowager house."

She pursed her lips. "I will come. In a fortnight, I will come to ensure the happiness of my daughter." Her eyes turned calculating, as if to warn them both.

Anne placed a hand on her arm. "Mother. I love you. I will do good with our name. And when Rosings Park is Darcy's, he shall care for it as if it were my own."

"Pardon?" Darcy looked from one to the other. "Did you say Rosings is to be mine?"

Lady Catherine turned furious eyes to him. "Yes, my dolt of a husband left it to you—not to Anne, you." She pointed a long bony finer at his chest.

"We will certainly care for Anne. And for Rosings." He shook his head. "Aunt, you would do far better to trust and to love than to manipulate and cajole. All will be well."

She spun on her heels, shrieking for servants to attend her, and at last left them in peace.

"That was a lot of information to take on at once."

Anne placed a sympathetic hand on his arm. Her eyes were wide and immediately filled with tears.

"Will you really find a position for Rolf?"

"Of course, Anne." He took her hands in his. "I wish for your every happiness."

"And I yours. Do you think you can win Elizabeth over to this crazy family?"

"I can only hope. I will get you settled at Pemberley and then ride in haste to Longbourn."

"Perhaps send a letter on ahead?"

"No time. I wish to be away from Rosings within the hour." He turned and beckoned to the servants. "Please see that my trunks are also packed."

When he returned to his room, his valet was already carefully filling his first trunk.

Darcy nodded and sat at a writing desk. He would write letters after all. One to a man of the church, inquiring after available positions, one to Mr. Bennet, and one to Miss Elizabeth herself.

Chapter Thirty-Three

Elizabeth drank in the fresh smells of the lovely trees lining the roads through Derbyshire. The rugged rocks, the hills, the brilliant water, and the trees were everything Lizzy most loved in the out of doors. She anxiously awaited their arrival so she could explore much by foot as well as carriage. The air had a slight chill, which felt refreshing to her as she tried to let as much of the crispness inside their carriage as possible.

"Whoa, girl." The driver stopped the horses. In a moment, he was peering his head in the window. "We are coming up on the largest estate in the area. Would you be wanting to turn in for a tour before we continue on our way?"

Lizzy's aunt leaned her head out the window. "Are we near Pemberley?"

"Yes, ma'am, we are. And I know the housekeeper is keen on doing the tours. They welcome visitors."

Her aunt's eyes glossed with happiness, while Lizzy's stomach flipped and turned with anxious anticipation. Surely Darcy was not home. No one would know she'd come. When her aunt and uncle turned to her for approval of the idea, she nodded. "Yes, let's see it."

They approached slowly, around a bend lined with trees, and then the house came into view. Lizzy's hand went to her heart. She had never seen anything so beautiful. It was a lovely house, and it felt like home. She could almost see Darcy standing on the top step. It was then she realized her error in wanting to come.

This visit would be torture of the purest form. This image of what might have been would remain in her brain forever. This coupled with Darcy's kisses and strength and intelligence, and she would never marry, for no one ever could measure up. It wasn't that the house was so large, though it was, nor was it that it sat so perfectly on the rise, which it did. Her attraction to the estate felt more personal. It simply felt like she belonged here.

Which she knew would sound so utterly presumptuous to anyone else. But she couldn't help what she felt. And it brought her the greatest pain. Wincing, she couldn't look away.

"Are you all right, Lizzy?" Her aunt's concerned voice warmed her.

"Yes, I'm well. This is quite the house, isn't it?"

"Indeed it is. And from what I remember, the kindest family. All the folks in town were grateful to them."

Lizzy could only nod in response as her first love became even more grand, while still forbidden to her. She sighed. Did she wish she'd never known him? She did not. Somehow even though her life would never be the same, she was happy he was a part of it, even if only in memory.

They approached the long drive and were soon welcomed into the house by a stately butler. He was tall and had a cheerful twinkle in his eye, even though his expression was appropriately blank. "I'll summon the housekeeper for a tour. If you could wait right here, please."

Lizzy wandered to a small bust of Darcy in an alcove along the wall. She sucked in a breath. "This is stunning."

"It certainly is, and I hear a good likeness." Her aunt's voice in her ear made her jump.

The housekeeper entered at that moment and began to take them around the home. Every room was tastefully appointed. Every room was lovely. She could see herself in every space. But the more they wandered, the more she knew this estate was more for people like Lady Anne. It was for the titled or the wealthy, or at least those with experience running large estates. She would be far from her abilities in attempting such a thing. How foolish she was to allow herself to fall in love with the only impossible man of her acquaintance.

They made their way through one room after another until they found themselves upstairs. Beautiful piano music filtered down the hall.

The housekeeper smiled. "And that would be Georgiana. We must make our way back downstairs so as not to disturb her practicing. But we're all real proud of her. She's quite proficient, isn't she?"

"It's the loveliest thing I've heard." Elizabeth smiled. "She has a real talent for playing with emotion."

"Are you someone who appreciates music, then?" The housekeeper smiled in return. "We could perhaps see if she would be willing to play a piece for you?"

Elizabeth was shaking her head before the finish of the question. "We mustn't. I would never wish to intrude." She turned toward the back stairwell. But the music had stopped and a voice carried down the hall. "Who is here?"

"Oh, we're sorry to disturb you, miss. I'm doing a tour, and they were so enamored with your music, we paused before descending."

Elizabeth turned with an apologetic smile. Georgiana was lovely, small boned, wide eyes, blond hair, with a gentle face and hands. Lizzy bobbed a quick curtsy. "We are sorry to intrude, miss."

"Oh, it is no bother." She curtsied as well. "In truth, I am hoping for a bit of company while I wait for my brother."

Alarm bells sounded in Elizabeth's ears. "Is he coming?"

She had squeaked out such an inappropriate question, she wished to run for the stairs, but there was nothing for it.

"He is indeed. And it has been many weeks since I've seen him. Would you come in?" Georgiana stepped back.

The housekeeper smiled encouragingly at them all, and Elizabeth could only accept. "Of course. Thank you."

"Do you play?" Georgiana indicated the piano.

"A bit, and very poorly, but I could turn your pages."

"Nonsense. We shall find a duet."

"Oh, I don't know that I could do your beautiful playing justice."

"I'm sure you could. Now, please, we must be introduced. Do you mind terribly that we have not been?"

"I do not." She curtsied again. "I am Elizabeth Bennet, and this is my aunt and uncle, Mr. and Mrs. Gardiner."

She placed a hand at her mouth. "Miss Elizabeth! My brother did not tell me you were coming. Goodness, I would have prepared something, anything. Mrs. Reynolds, could we get a tea tray with some of the cook's finest biscuits, and whatever else they can muster up for someone truly special?" Georgiana shook her head. "I am terribly sorry."

Baffled, completely confused, Elizabeth reached out a hand to place on top of her wringing ones. "Please. I do not understand. I am no one special. We were in the area and stopped by on our tour of Derbyshire. It is my understanding that Mr. Darcy is still at Rosings . . ."

Georgiana shook her head. "No, he isn't. He is arriving straightaway, and with Lady Anne as well. From what I understand, you were a large part of her agreeing to come." She glanced at the Gardiners. "But I am sorry to divulge family details in so careless a manner."

"No, not to worry, of course. I am flattered your brother would have spoken of me at all," Elizabeth said.

Georgiana smiled a sisterly grin and murmured close to her ear, "He did more than simply speak of you. I have heard many mentions and specific details. You are a lady to be admired, he said. A woman of great wit. And he mentioned your talent on the pianoforte. He greatly enjoyed hearing you play."

Elizabeth shook her head again. There had been a brief moment at the dinner party when she'd been prevailed upon to play. "I cannot account for it, any of it." When Georgiana looked troubled, she put an arm around her shoulders. "But that isn't to say I do not greatly admire your brother. He is the best of men. I was just afraid I might never see him again. I planned on such a sadness and have been at this very moment attempting to find a way to put him from my mind."

She felt her eyes well up. "And to hear you speak of me." She waved her hands, trying unsuccessfully to stop the tears. "I cannot allow your words to give me hope. I cannot. For it is time to let him go." She placed a hand over her mouth and looked away, but there was no hiding her emotion. As embarrassed as she was, there was nothing for it.

But Georgiana embraced her and whispered in her ear, "I don't think you have anything to fear here. He is most enamored with you. He can speak of nothing else."

"But Lady Anne . . . I could never ruin her happiness."

Georgiana kept shaking her head. She pulled away and put two hands on either of Elizabeth's shoulders. Staring her straight in the face, she laughed. "Nothing to worry about there either, I assure you."

Georgiana's expression was so sincere. She seemed to be telling the truth. She was so pleased to be with Elizabeth. She was such a dear. Elizabeth wondered just what Darcy had told her. The fact that he'd mentioned her at all to his sister was a good sign. At least that's what Elizabeth could only hope at this moment. But then she gasped. "You said he's coming here now?"

Georgiana giggled. "I expect him at any moment."

Her heart leapt to her throat. "Then we must leave straightaway!" She turned to tug at her aunt's sleeve.

The Gardiners, who up until this moment had stood and watched the entire interchange, now shook their heads. "Elizabeth. Surely you don't mean that."

"Oh, I do. We mustn't be here when he arrives." She sucked in a breath. "At all. We must not be here." She hurried from the room and down the hall, but when she turned back, the Gardiners were not with her. She retraced her steps, only to find them chatting happily with Georgiana. And then just as she was about to usher them from the room, Darcy stepped around the corner in the hall.

He stopped short as soon as he saw her, his face completely blank.

Completely mortified, Elizabeth curtsied, eyes on the floor. "Mr. Darcy."

"Miss Elizabeth . . ."

The silence lasted a moment too long. She looked up.

Darcy stood just where he had, his face still a mask. But then Georgiana stepped out into the hall. "I thought I heard you. Brother! Isn't it wonderful Elizabeth has come to call?!" She hugged him.

He wrapped his arms around her. "It is good to see you. How are you?"

"Most excellent, and pleased to have met her. Come, meet her aunt and uncle."

As Georgiana tugged her brother back into the sitting area, he glanced over his shoulder at her and smiled. That smile—normal, happy, expecting good things—undid a portion of the tightness in her chest.

So she followed him in, unsure exactly how any of this would play out. But she watched as Georgiana introduced her beloved aunt and uncle to the man of her dreams. And all she could do was smile.

Darcy clasped their hands warmly and smiled into their

faces. "I am so pleased you have come. How long are you in the area?"

"Well, we haven't decided. We'd hoped to spend some time here in Derbyshire, as my wife grew up here and has many fond memories," her uncle said.

"Then you will most definitely be welcome to come fish in our ponds and to use our property as your own. Where are you staying?"

"The inn in town."

"You must come and stay here. We will have the rooms readied for your use." He turned to Elizabeth then, with a question in his eyes. "If you would like?"

Her aunt and uncle turned hopeful expressions to her. Georgiana gave her an encouraging smile. Elizabeth stepped closer to Darcy. All she could see in his face was the same hope, with a warmth that sent fire to her toes. She nodded. "I'd like that very much."

With a quick nod, he waved a hand to the waiting maid. "Please see that the Yellow Room is readied for Miss Elizabeth, and Mr. and Mrs. Gardiner can be next door."

"Very good, sir." The maid hurried from the room.

"I didn't know you would be here," Elizabeth told Darcy.

"You came, not knowing you would see me?"

"Of course. I could never stop by unannounced, not when . . ." Aware that they had an audience, she simply shrugged. "It feels very untoward."

"Not at all. I cannot tell you how pleased I am you are here."

"We were about to attempt a duet." Georgiana smiled and waved Elizabeth over to the piano.

"And here is where I embarrass myself, surely." She swished her skirts. "But I shan't allow myself to be intimidated. I will simply smile and play." She laughed. When Georgiana sat beside her, she swallowed. "I am really not very good. Perhaps you can help cover for me?"

"Of course, but I won't belive you aren't. Fitzwilliam never tells a falsehood."

"I believe that to be true. Then he is too kind in his view of me."

"He does think only good things, it seems." Georgiana nudged her. "And I can see why. I'm so pleased you will be with us. I long to know you better."

"I as well. And thank you." Elizabeth could hardly believe this sudden change of fortune. She didn't quite know what to think or do. But as she met Darcy's gaze, he winked and then smiled encouragingly. So perhaps all would be well. Perhaps. It was a powerful word, and laced with hope.

They chose a simple but beautiful duet which allowed them to sing, beginning straightaway.

When the time came, Darcy approached to turn the page. He leaned over her, his body pressed against her back, and then he rested a hand on her shoulder.

"I shall not allow you to intimidate me, sir."

He chuckled behind her, then leaned forward. "You play beautifully."

She felt her face heat, but there was nothing for it. She could no sooner control her reactions to Darcy than the rising of the moon.

When they were finished, the tea tray had arrived. And it was full of an assortment of delicacies. Tarts, biscuits, jams, sandwiches, all presented in such a lovely manner that Elizabeth hesitated to disturb anything.

"Come now, we must have tea." Georgiana asked them all to sit. Darcy and Elizabeth shared a small sofa. Her aunt and uncle took chairs next to Miss Georgiana, and she poured the tea. She did an excellent job, and when she was finished, she looked to Darcy for approval. He smiled in return and his sister beamed. Elizabeth decided theirs was the sweetest sibling relationship, and she immediately missed Jane.

Georgiana seemed to notice Elizabeth's approval, because she said, "I have the best of brothers. He is too good and too kind. Since our parents passed, he has been nothing but gracious and patient with me." She ran her hand along the top of the piano. "He even purchased this piano for me."

Mrs. Gardiner appropriately gushed over such a gesture. And Elizabeth couldn't have been more enamored with the whole experience.

And then Anne walked in the room.

"Oh!" She stood. "Lady Anne, hello." An awkwardness settled in the air around Elizabeth, which she did not know how to dispel.

"Miss Elizabeth." Anne held out her hands to welcome her, so she stepped closer and they clasped hands. Anne leaned in and kissed her cheek. "We are so pleased you would come."

We? Elizabeth didn't know what to make of the situation. Why was Anne here? Was she moving in to be Darcy's wife? Did she consider herself the hostess? She was definitely more a part of Pemberley than Elizabeth herself was. She kissed Georgiana, and soon the two were thick together in a girly chatter that left Elizabeth completely at odds.

Darcy smiled at the two of them for a moment while the Gardiners and Elizabeth shared looks that read: *Perhaps it is time for us to leave?*

But Darcy soon rested a hand on top of Elizabeth's. "Should we send the servants after your belongings?"

"Oh, well, yes, that would be lovely, but might I speak with you a moment?" She indicated the hall.

He stood. "Certainly."

As soon as they were out of earshot, she reached for his arm. "You must know I did not come thinking to find you here."

"I wish you had. I'm not sure I understand why you'd

wish to avoid me . . . Do you wish to avoid me?" The insecurity in his expression warmed and strengthened her.

"No, of course not. I mean, earlier, when I thought I'd never see you again, I'd hoped to avoid you so as to ease the pain of being apart. I didn't think we had a chance to be together. And now?" She tipped her head toward the room. "With Anne? Do you think it appropriate for us to also stay here? I would not wish to interrupt anything." She stumbled over her words. They came out slower than she anticipated. But she didn't know what to say, what to ask to discover her place in this house, to know Anne's place in Darcy's life.

"Anne is here at my request. We are both very happy to have her and to free her from her mother. I think it will be good for her."

Elizabeth nodded. "I can see that."

Darcy studied her. "But you feel uncomfortable."

"Naturally. If you two are attempting to discover—if you wish to court her—oh, this is terribly awkward. I simply do not wish to stand in your way."

"You don't?" His eyes twinkled.

"Oh stop. You must not tease me in this moment."

"I know. I'm sorry. It is terribly unfair of me. But Elizabeth—might I call you that?"

She nodded.

"I have no intentions of marrying Anne."

Elizabeth's mouth went dry with happiness. Was such a thing possible? She tried to swallow. "Does Anne know?"

He tipped his head back to laugh. "She most certainly does." He tugged on his suit coat. "In fact, a certain man named Rolf and his children will be arriving any day." His face beamed with happiness, and it was all Elizabeth could do not to throw herself into his arms. "Oh, Darcy. You are the best of me."

Great relief washed through her. "Well then, as for the rest, we shall just have to see, then, won't we?"

His eyes turned knowing and his smile wiggled at the corner. "What more do we need to know, my dearest Elizabeth? I am at last free to act in a manner most designed for my happiness, and I intend to do just that. Tomorrow will be the first day of many."

"And what do you plan to do with this new search for happiness?"

He shook his head slowly. "I did not say search. I said act. I have found my happiness."

"You have?" She held her breath.

"Yes, and now I just need to court her properly so that she may decide if I am hers."

She nodded, and decided that instead of telling him outright that she already knew he was her everything, she wanted a bit of that courting he was talking about. So she just smiled and said, "I think I like the sound of that."

"I figured you might. Shall we begin at breakfast? Picnic on the lawn?"

"I'd love that."

"And then a ride out to the back pastures?"

"On Samson?"

"If you wish."

"I wish."

His grin widened. "And then a swim in the back pond . . ."

His expression turned daring, so she didn't even flinch. "Excellent."

"I think I've found the perfect women as well as happiness."

"Oh, I'm not perfect, believe me. I have all kinds of flaws. You will wish to toss me out half the time you want to kiss me. I hope you will want to kiss me." She felt her face heat, and then looked away. "I am too bold."

He lifted her hand to his mouth and kissed the tips of her gloved fingers. "I like you bold."

She lifted her gaze to his. "Then you might like this?" She quirked an eyebrow, went up on the tips of her toes, and pressed her lips to his.

His eyebrows shot up, but he softened his lips against hers and held her a moment longer than she had planned before letting her go. "I like bold indeed." His grin made her laugh.

"What are you laughing about out there?" Anne peeked her head out the door.

"Oh, I'm just setting up a courting schedule with our guest."

"At long last, Darcy in love. This is going to be most entertaining." Anne's eyes twinkled, but she stepped back into the room.

"I like her."

"She's a different person when not with her mother."

"I see that." Elizabeth tucked her hand into his arm. "And now we must return to the others. I long to know your dear Georgiana better."

"And she you. But wait a moment more."

She turned to face him.

His gaze traveled over her face, her lips, her eyes, down her neck, and back to her eyes again. His face softened and he leaned closer, his expression full of sincerity. "In case there is ever any wonder or worry, you are the only woman I have ever wanted to stand at my side here at Pemberley. And it's not because you are perfect, though I have yet to find a fault. It is simply because I have fallen in love with you and wish to spend every moment at your side."

She found it difficult to inhale the next breath. Her eyes welled with tears and she tried a wobbly smile. When she could speak, she blinked back the tears and said, "I love you too. All I've ever wanted since our first meeting is to be with you."

"Then let's not leave each other's side from this moment on. I shall allow sleep in a room close to mine, but otherwise we are to be together."

"Perhaps an hour or two could be spared for your business and my aunt and uncle?"

"Yes, fine. But then together." He laughed. "You are more than enough, my dear sweet Elizabeth. And I cannot wait to prove my devotion to you."

They stepped into the room. And they had the loveliest evening, telling stories of their youth and enjoying each other's company until it was long past time to sleep.

When Elizabeth entered her rooms, she was delighted at the walls, the bed, the furniture and what promised to be a glorious view. Her trunk had arrived and her clothes were unpacked into her closet. A maid waited to help her dress. She fell sleep under the softest covers, asking if this could all really be her life.

Chapter Thirty-Four

Darcy asked for an assortment of the most delicious breakfast foods Cook could make. Then he paced mercilessly outside the kitchen doors until the staff were all a nervous wreck. He moved to the main hall, staring up the staircase, hoping to see her descend. Twenty of the longest minutes later, he jumped at the first sight of her.

She wore an emerald-green morning dress. Her brilliant eyes flashed at him as she made her way down the stairs.

He waited only until she had reached halfway, then he took the steps two at a time to reach her and offer his arm for the rest of the descent.

"It's lovely to see you, Mr. Darcy, how did you sleep?"

"Excellent." He cleared his throat, his eyes sheepish. "Terribly."

"Oh dear."

"I kept wondering at the time, hoping it was already morning and I would again see you." He wiped a hand down his face. "Perhaps that is not the thing to admit. But it is true nonetheless."

"Oh my dear, I think I have the solution."

"And what is that?"

"You must spend your sleeping hours dreaming of me as I did you." Her cheeks blushed furiously, and he found it quite delightful.

"How charming of you to admit such a thing."

"It is wonderfully and embarrassingly true. You were the subject of all my dreams. My hero in each one. It was an endless romance novel, and I quite enjoyed myself."

He felt inordinately proud of himself for her dreams even though he had nothing whatsoever to do with them. "I'm pleased to hear it. I shall attempt to create such an experience for myself." He led her to the kitchen. "And now we must collect our breakfast and our horse." He laughed. "Are you certain you do not wish to ride your own horse?"

"I think I'd better begin with my own, but I know I'll wish the entire time that I could mount Samson with you. It will be so unfair."

"Then we shall enjoy ourselves immensely, and I'll take you out to the back corner of the property to one of my favorite places in the world. And perhaps we'll enjoy a time together on the same horse." He grinned.

"I'd very much like to see it, this favorite spot of yours."

She looked all around them. "I'd like to see all that you love here. I want to know everything about you, about Pemberley, about your servants."

He laughed. "Even the servants!" The nearest footman stood perfectly still, but his mouth twitched. Elizabeth noticed and turned to him with victory-filled eyes. "Proud of making Thomas almost smile?"

The servant seemed to stiffen, to hold the blankest expression possible.

"I would be too. He is very well trained. But I happen to know that when he's down in the kitchen, he's the one with the most sense of humor."

"Is he now? Well, I can see that, especially if he can appreciate my comments. Perhaps we should join the servants in the kitchen a time or two."

Darcy's eyebrows rose. "Would you like that?"

"I would indeed."

He nodded. "Done. We shall do it after I have fully impressed you with all Pemberley has to offer one it loves." His eyes widened. What had he just admitted again and in such a carefree way?

"I will never tire of hearing that. And if your estate also loves me, I shall find much happiness here, I do believe."

"I hope for that more than most other things." He offered his arm. Servants followed with their picnic, and he lead her out to the barn.

Once they were up on horses and riding out across the

meadow, he turned to her with a daring expression, "Now, Lizzy."

Her cheeks colored and he grinned.

"How about that race?"

Before he could count off or say anything more, she'd dug in her heel and was tearing out across the meadow.

"Confound the woman. She's going in the wrong direction." He laughed to himself and could feel the expectant hum of Samson beneath him. "Go after her before she does something she'll regret."

The horse shuddered a moment and then leapt forward. Soon he was neck and neck with the beautiful Elizabeth Bennet, and he didn't think anything in the world could be better than riding with her out across his property.

He directed them both toward the river and softer land near the back corner, and soon they were meandering along a private, picturesque section of trees.

The servants had laid out the picnic before their arrival. And Elizabeth's face was all the reward he needed. She spun around the small grove with hands at the sides of her face. "I can see why this would be a favorite. It's one of the loveliest places in all the world."

He nodded. "Made even more so by your presence." He'd not brought anyone else to this spot, though he'd come here often as a boy and then as he'd grown. He spent a long morning here the day after his father died. It was his place of comfort, his place of inspiration, his place of solace. And now it would become his place of memories, of love.

He held out a hand. "Walk with me."

She readily laced their fingers together and he led her toward the river. "There is a spot in here I'd like to show you." He stooped to pick up several twigs and leaves from the ground. And when they were at the banks of a slow, meandering stream, he handed her a handful of them. "Let's see what happens when we toss in a leaf or two, shall we?"

She placed hers carefully on the surface and watched as it spun and whirled and made its way downstream. He did the same, and then they threw in twigs and more leaves, anything they thought would carry.

He nodded. "At Pemberley, the things we do matter. It is as if we are sending our actions, our words, our thoughts, even, down the stream. They will be seen and noted and often followed."

She nodded, watching him.

"It matters very much to me who I have at my side." His mouth twitched. "Not just for my own happiness, but because there are such far-reaching effects of those who represent Pemberley."

Her face clouded with worry, and she looked away. "I am afraid I'm a far cry from what you would need here, Darcy. We might make each other happy temporarily, but in the long run, I'm afraid you will wish me gone." She turned from him, her shoulders slumping.

Stunned at her reaction, he found his thoughts scrambled for a moment, at a loss of what to say. How could she not know how absolutely perfect she was for him?

He tugged her hand. "No, not at all. Miss Elizabeth, please. My words are having the opposite effect I intended." His chest tightened with concern. What evidence had he ever given her that she was valuable to him? That he cared? "Up until this moment, I have treated you abominably."

She started to shake her head, but he held up a hand. "Please allow me to attempt to explain. I don't think there is anything I can say that will make it right. But to think that I held you at a distance, that I engaged in flirtations, that I kissed you, all the while not willing to give up everything for you, not willing to show you just how valuable you are to me." He swallowed the painful lump in his throat. "If I am able, I will spend every day for the rest of my life trying to prove to you that I was a complete imbecile and that I would only be lucky to win your hand now."

He paused. That went further than he'd planned in this exact moment. He brushed off his coat. "You have not been to London for a Season and therefore might not know, but you are a true diamond among anyone I could meet and marry there." He lifted her hand in his and began tugging off her gloves. "You are exactly what I need, exactly what Pemberley needs, and there is nothing, no one, I will ever see or meet that could possibly convince me otherwise."

She shook her head. "I can promise you I would try. I

would work hard to be what you need here. But would we be truly happy?"

He stepped closer, lifted her glove-free hand to his mouth, and pressed his lips to her knuckles, one at a time, his lips caressing her skin, his mouth moving over her hand until he could hardly stand the distance to her mouth. But he waited. He cleared some hair from off her brow. "Lizzy."

She closed her eyes and smiled. "I love it when you call me that."

"My dearest Lizzy. Will you marry me?"

Her eyes shot open.

But he held her gaze; he filled her with all the love he could possibly muster in one look and nodded his head. "Marry me, Lizzy. Make me the happiest of men. Bless all our lives. Please." He waited. He watched her.

She took time considering him. Her eyes lit as though discovering something truly magical. But she waited. She tipped her head, and then a large smile spread across her full lips. "Yes. I promised myself to act only in accordance with my own best chance for happiness. And you, Mr. Darcy, are the joy of my life. Yes. I'll marry you and I'll do my best to be what Pemberley needs." She lifted up onto her toes. "But I do suspect I might have what Mr. Darcy needs already."

"Do you?"

She nodded. "I do." Then she lifted her mouth to him, pulled him down to her, and kissed him with all the love she could muster. When his hands wrapped around her back and sat at her waist, she melted into him. He responded with a gentleness and persistence that pulled her closer, melted her insides, and made her ask for more, more, forever more of Mr. Darcy.

He could not believe his good fortune, could not believe he had almost missed a life with Elizabeth, could not believe he held her in his arms and could do so again whenever they wished for such a thing. His lips toyed with hers, pressing and teasing and then he held her close with earnest. He loved this woman. He loved her with everything he could. His heart ached with the love and for the first time since he'd lost his parents, a piece of him felt healed, another piece felt whole and he knew that he and Georgiana had again found a family.

After a time, too short a time, he pulled away, lifted her hands up again to his mouth, and said, "I have a box of precious things. In it are three rings—you may choose which one you like or we can use one of the stones in our vault to set at the jeweler."

She nodded. "I'm sure I will love anything that means I'm married to you." She kissed his knuckles in return, a quick cascade of happiness since they were right there, close to them both. "Thank you."

"Hmm?" He smiled.

"Thank you for loving me."

He bent his shoulder and lifted her up into his arms. "You must never thank me for doing something so profound as loving you. How could I not? It is I who thank you for agreeing to marry this sorry sap of a dancer, this lowly, poor communicator, this man who cannot come up with an engaging sentence for strangers. Thank you for binding your life to mine. I shall be blessed every day because of it." He spun her around and then lifted her up on his horse. "And now I think it is time we both rode Samson for a bit."

The friendly horse's nickers made her laugh. And his arms around her warmed her toes. "Do you know what, Mr. Darcy?"

"What is that?"

"I think we shall both be very happy."

He nudged the horse, who leapt in response. As Lizzy's shouts echoed across the meadow, he could only agree. "I do believe you are right." He nuzzled her neck and placed a kiss just below her ear. "Starting right now."

She leaned back up against him even though they were riding at breakneck speed. He wrapped his arms around her and let the horse take them wherever he led.

The End.

For a sneak peek at the next Jane Austen adaptation, join my newsletter. Follow her Newsletter

Follow Jen

Jen's other published books

The Duke's Second Chance
The Earl's Winning Wager
Her Lady's Whims and Whimsies
Suitors for the Proper Miss
Pining for Lord Lockhart
The Foibles and Follies of Miss Grace

The Nobleman's Daughter
Two lovers in disguise

Scarlet
The Pimpernel retold

A Lady's Maid

Can she love again?

His Lady in Hiding
Hiding out as his maid.

Spun of Gold
Rumpelstilskin Retold

Dating the Duke
Time Travel: Regency man in NYC

Charmed by His Lordship
The antics of a fake friendship

Tabitha's Folly
Four over-protective brothers

To read Damen's Secret
The Villain's Romance

Follow her Newsletter

www.ingramcontent.com/pod-product-compliance
Lightning Source LLC
Chambersburg PA
CBHW071425260626
47170CB00008B/2595

9781737592198